MW01378747

For Kathy,

Nice to meet you!

Jessie M.

Issym 2

Issym

Book One of the Xsardis Chronicles

By Jessie Mae Hodsdon

Adventure with a purpose

Issym 4

ISBN 978-0-9843386-0-3

Cover Art by Lina Torosyan

Published by Rebirth Publishing, Inc.

Printed in the United States

Visit www.issym.com

Acknowledgements:

How can I properly thank everyone who has helped me? I have needed every prayer, every encouraging word and every smile that anyone who has ever met me has given me!

To my editors: Judy, Julie, Kate and Stephani—without you this really would never have come to be.

To my amazing illustrator: Lina—I truly appreciate all that you have done. Your patience and your vision for the project have been key.

To my family: thanks for believing in me. You have been a great support team.

And to God: You make the impossible, possible. You make strength out of my weakness. You have given victory where I only saw defeat. Praise Your Name forever!

Issym 6

For Kate, my dear friend and loved sister

Issym

8

Introduction:

Joppa gave a sigh of relief as he put down his feather pen. It had taken a long time to compile the tale, but he was finally finished.

"Are you done, Uncle?" asked the eleven-year-old girl, who sat reading beside him.

He nodded his head. Joppa feared that she was too old for him to read to her, but he asked anyway, "Would you like to hear it?"

"Yes please," she replied as she set her book down and moved closer to him, resting her head on her arms in his lap. The girl looked up at him expectantly and lovingly.

Joppa was a keeper of pure, unembellished history. Only a few months ago a man came from the neighboring continent of Issym, telling tales and bearing scrolls as proof, of a recent, marvelous adventure. Joppa rarely got information from Issym and therefore spent most of his time recording the events of his home continent, Asandra. It had been with great joy that the old man had received the scrolls from across the sea. Immediately he had begun the task of discerning the truth between the many different accounts told on paper and by the visitor. It was for this true account of Issym that his niece had been waiting.

Looking down at the curly haired girl, he saw that her eyes were full of excitement as he opened the book he had worked so hard on. Joppa was glad the tale would distract her from the coming destruction—for a little while at least. The old man simply hoped he would get to the end of the story before the intruders came. He knew it would not be long before the so-called queen discovered his home.

Joppa took a breath and told his niece, "The story actually begins hundreds of years ago." He then started to read...

"As you know on our planet, Xsardis, there are two continents: Issym and Asandra. They are named after two great people. I will tell you their tale.

"Issym lived in the domain of King Shobal, on the continent that would later be named after him. The king was a good man who ruled his people well. Issym was brave of heart, skilled with the sword and great in knowledge. He wandered from place to place in the kingdom of Shobal, rescuing the innocent and punishing the evil. He was a legend—told as bedtime stories to children.

"One day while Issym was walking through the woods next to the ocean he saw a long-boat coming from a ship that was flying an unknown flag. In the vessel were three men and a woman whose hands were bound. The craft landed and one of the men exited the boat, followed by the other two, dragging their captive. Her long, curly, red hair was matted, her arms were bruised and her dress was torn. Issym realized that this woman had been kidnapped, and without hesitating, ran toward them—silently and swiftly—a sword drawn in one hand and a knife in the other.

"One of the ruffians saw Issym when he was halfway to the boat. Issym threw his knife at the kidnapper to silence him from warning the ship waiting in the harbor; the blade found its target in his throat. The fallen man's cohorts saw him collapse, and were alerted of Issym's presence. One of them kept a tight hold on the lady's arm while the other let go of her and prepared to face Issym.

"Issym crossed the distance between them in seconds, killing the first attacker with one swing of his sword and the second with two. Before he could introduce himself to the lady he had rescued, he saw a second long boat mere yards from the shore. The hero knew that they had to get far away from the beach. With a quick flash of his blade, he freed the woman's bound wrists and the two started to run for the woods. With his gleaming sword he cut away anything that stood in their path.

"He did not have to look behind him to know they were being followed—he heard their pursuers' footsteps and shouting voices. The woman he had set free ran after him, letting him lead her. They hurried to the densest part of the woods. He dropped to the ground, and the lady followed his example, as he pulled some bushes over them for cover.

"The hero and the maiden caught their breath, but said nothing until the sailors had passed. Then the wandering warrior gave the lady his name, 'I am Issym.'

"'Asandra,' she replied. While they walked to the closest village Asandra told him that she had been kidnapped from her kingdom across the sea, because she was of royal blood, and asked the swordsman to take her back to her people. As he looked into her eyes, he knew he could not refuse her.

"They sailed back to her continent and traveled to the castle, which was her home. The journey took several months and during that time the hero and the lady fell in love.

"On arriving at the castle Asandra learned that the men who had captured her had also murdered her father. Issym tracked down the men and avenged the king. When he returned to the castle, he and Asandra were married and for five years lived happily together as king and queen.

"After that time Issym received word from King Shobal. The king had heard stories of his former subject's heroism and informed Issym that his home continent was being attacked. He asked for the warrior's help. Issym was loath to leave Asandra but she told him he should go. He heeded his bride's counsel and returned to the place of his birth.

"For years Asandra did not hear from her champion, and she began to fear that he had died. Despite her concerns she ruled her people well in Issym's absence. The queen was fair and wise. Her subjects adored her, and she governed them justly, working hard to improve their lives. Anyone and everyone was welcome in her home.

"Finally Issym returned victorious and with a debt of gratitude from Shobal. The people of the kingdom rejoiced at his homecoming, but none so much as his beloved Asandra. For many more years they lived happily, as Asandra ruled the people with her wise heart, and Issym protected them with his mighty hand. These were happy times for all, until the cherished queen, Asandra, died. Issym mourned her deeply, for their love had surpassed all others. Living among her people, the distraught warrior could not escape the memory of his wife, so he bade the kingdom farewell. They wept to see him go, and gave him a gift they knew he would cherish forever... They named their continent Asandra.

"Issym returned to the land of his birth and sat at Shobal's right hand, continuing to fight whenever there was a need. When Shobal died, he left the kingdom to Issym. He ruled well and his people loved him, for he had saved them from many evils.

"The people of Issym's kingdom had heard of what those across the sea had done when their queen had been taken from them by death. When Issym passed, they named their continent after him.

"That was the story of Issym and Asandra," Joppa declared, looking down at his niece. "Now I shall tell you what happened in the land of Issym long after that tale took place."

Chapter 1

Thunder rippled across the frozen lake. Water sheeted from the blackened sky, banging on the windows and roof of the costly house. Bolt after bolt of lightning struck, brightening up the world for less than a second and then leaving it in greater darkness than before.

Tension reigned in the house's living room. Another bolt of lightning flashed, and the thunder that followed was so loud the teen could barely hear the four-year-olds' high pitched screams. The twin girls buried their faces in her shoulder and lap. The sitter liked rain, and even enjoyed thunder, but not when she was the sole semi-grown-up in a big, empty house. Her imagination ran away with her—wasn't this the same scenario every horror movie that she refused to watch started with? She shook her head. Her charges were sobbing. She needed to act like an adult. "Mary, Elise, do you know where lightning comes from?" she began.

The identical faces looked up at her. "No, Rachel," they declared in unison.

Rachel whispered, "Water sprites," thinking up a story as quickly as she could.

"Water sprites?" Mary asked, sniffling and not letting go of Rachel's arm.

"They are a little shorter than you, with slender bodies and beautiful wings, although they can only fly short distances. They control the water. They only use lightning and thunder when they are very happy or very unhappy."

"They must be very unhappy!" cried Elise, the more emotional twin.

"Oh no," Rachel replied. "Tonight, they are extremely happy. The lightning is their fireworks." The girls were drying their tears. The teen continued, "Once, there was a young, poor water sprite whose name was Lucas. He fell in love with a slave named Lilly. Because Lilly was so beautiful and smart, her mistress, Tamar, hated her and refused to give her in marriage to Lucas."

"Oh!" gasped Mary and Elise, now absorbed in Rachel's story and ignoring the storm raging outside.

Rachel took a breath to go on, but stopped short. What was that smell? She shrugged and went on, "Lucas loved Lilly too much to give up. He thought that if he could find enough money to buy Lilly's freedom he could marry her. So Lucas flew to the water and there signed up with a ship that was in search of buried treasure. But the boat got caught in a storm and Lucas almost died! He flew to an island and there lived for many days, sure that he would starve."

"No... he can't die. What about Lilly?" Elise protested. "What happened to her?"

"A vessel flying a black flag appeared near an island. It was a pirate ship. And guess who was held captive by the pirates?"

"Lilly?" Elise suggested.

"Tamar," Mary declared.

"Tamar," Rachel confirmed.

"Lucas hid when the pirates landed. They made camp and posted just one guard for Tamar. He fell asleep. Lucas flew to her and said, 'I've come to rescue you.' But Tamar tried to refuse his help. She was a very sour sprite."

"What happened?" Elise needed to know. "Did they get caught?"

"No. Lucas succeeded in getting Tamar onto the ship and together they sailed back to her home. When they arrived, the whole community hailed him as a hero but Tamar wanted to have him killed."

"But he had saved her," Mary could not believe it.

"Tamar hated work and Lucas had needed her help sailing the ship. He had forced her to tie the riggings and steer the boat. So, even though he had rescued her, she was really mad at him."

"Did... did Lucas die?" Elise's eyes filled again with tears.

"The community refused to listen to Tamar. They offered Lucas anything he wanted. He asked for Lilly's freedom. Today they were married. And they wanted to celebrate so they lit up the sky with lightning and made it known for miles with the thunder."

The girls sat for a moment and then Mary, realizing that the tale was over, said, "Your stories are so good, Rachel."

"Thank you," Rachel replied, not really thinking about what the girl had said. She was certain that she smelled something funny. Once she got the twins in bed, she was determined to find out what it was.

Another flash of lightning and the sound of thunder scared the girls. "Why don't we play one more game before I put you in bed?" the teen suggested.

"Three questions," Mary decided without consulting either Rachel or Elise. She began immediately, "Who was your first best friend?"

Rachel moved the kids towards their room as she answered, "His name was Seth. He was my next-door-neighbor when I was your age."

"Wha wash ee sike?" Mary responded, toothbrush still in her mouth.

"He had a good imagination. We would pretend that I was a princess locked in a dragon-guarded tower and that he was the knight who came to my rescue." She paused and then added, "That was your second question. Elise gets to ask the last one."

"Rachel!" Mary protested, washing out her toothbrush and joining Elise in their room.

Elise thought for a second as she pulled her nightshirt on. "Why aren't you at the party tonight? Our next-door-neighbor Missy is having a birthday party."

"Because I'm here."

"But *everyone* is going," Mary pointed out.

Rachel sighed. "If you must know, I wasn't invited."

"But you and Missy go to the same church... You should be at the party."

Rachel patted on the bed and Mary hopped onto it, laying beside her sister. The teen pulled the covers up. "Let me tell you something *real.*"

"Okay."

"Sometimes, when you do what is right, people don't like it."

"But..." Elise replied, "when you do something good you should get a reward. That's what Mom says."

"You should; but it doesn't always happen that way. Remember Jesus? He did lots of good things—miracles, healings and feeding large crowds. He was God's son, and perfect. But He was killed by the people He had tried to help."

"It's not fair," Mary decided.

"No," Rachel shook her head, "it's not. Now, no more questions. Time for bed."

"What about our story?"

"You've already had your story and its fifteen minutes past your bed time." Rachel kissed them both goodnight and turned off the light. Shutting the door behind her, she set out to find what was causing that smell. It reminded her of the smoke of her fireplace at home; but Mary and Elise's family used oil, not wood.

She moved through the living room. Was it just her imagination that the air seemed thick and foggy? Rachel put her hand on the doorknob leading to the kitchen. "Ouch!" she pulled back.

There was no burn on her hand, but the knob had felt scorching. Her mind raced. She moved towards another door to the kitchen. It was partially open and she pushed it.

The room was ablaze. Smoke poured into the living room so that she could barely see. Her lungs burned and her eyes watered. Rachel staggered backwards and ran into the twin's bedroom.

The living room was now on fire. She looked around her for anyway out of the house. She pulled and pushed on the bedroom's window. It would not budge.

The twins saw the fire and were screaming. Panic seized Rachel. That, and the smoke, brought on an asthma attack. It felt like she was breathing through a coffee stirrer. She banged on the window, knowing that time was short. Nothing happened. She felt herself falling.

Two sweaty teenage boys stepped into the house after finishing a game of basketball. The taller one, with dirty blond hair, heard the phone ringing and dove after it, but whoever it was had already hung up. "Who called, Seth?" asked the shorter one.

Seth checked the caller ID, "My mom again."

"Man she's worried about us! That's, what, the fifth time? Your parents have only been gone for a few hours. What did you tell her about me?"

"I said, 'Mom, Max is an ax murder, but he's trying to turn over a new leaf. Can he please come over?'" Seth paused while he dialed his mom back. "Hey, we were out playing basketball... No, we're fine... I promise... Mom, don't worry so much! Have a good time... Yes, I know... Okay. Bye."

Max looked at him with raised eyebrows, "Your parents are way too up tight. I don't know how you survive it. You'd think they'd relax a little while they're on their anniversary trip, at least."

"It's not normally like this. I've been at home alone many times," Seth attempted to regain a little pride. "But there have been a series of burglaries in this neighborhood."

That peaked Max's interest, "Really?"

"Just small stuff. People will come home and find the alarm system disabled and the TV on, but nothing missing. Or a few items gone, but many expensive ones left behind. Many of the crimes didn't get reported for a couple of days because the homeowners just thought they had misplaced their medicine or jewelry or something."

"Just how many break-ins have you guys had?" Max took a seat on a stool in the kitchen, the coolness of night having set in and darkness only a few moments away. It was eerie to talk about robberies alone in a house at night—almost like they were telling ghost stories.

"It's hard to tell for sure, but at least ten."

"I don't get that. If I was the burglar, I'd want to raid one house so well that I could retire from my life of crime, but moving around from house to house in the *same* neighborhood? That's just dumb."

"The police have been watching, but two more burglaries have still taken place. They've been in the paper. How come you haven't heard about them?"

"I don't waste time with newspapers and television. Video games are much more fun."

Video games had been Max's whole world from the time they had met. Max had been Seth's first New York friend. Seth had proudly brought Max to his new house, took him to his room and pulled out swords and bows and legos and Spiderman toys. "You play with those?" he had laughed

"Don't you?" Seth had asked him.

"No one our age does."

"Then what do you do?"

"Don't you have any video games?"

"One or two."

That was when the very fiber of Seth's being changed. He turned his attention from imagining stories to climbing the social ladder. And he succeeded. By his sophomore year of high school he was running the basketball team, leading a band and attending all the important parties. Whoever was his friend, was everyone's friend. Whatever he did, everyone did.

It was work to keep up his popularity. The danger of slipping off the top was much too great for him to risk correcting someone doing something wrong or sticking up for a kid getting picked on. He tried back door avenues of doing the right thing, but sometimes he wondered if he had lost his backbone.

"Did you order the pizza yet?" Max asked.

As they began a movie, they devoured their meatlovers pizza, complimentary bag of chips and bottle of soda. Conversation died out as the movie went on, until finally, at the exact same moment, both boys fells in to a deep, unnatural sleep.

Chapter 2

Seth was the first to wake up; he wondered why he was so cold. The teen opened his eyes, expecting to see his living room ceiling, but what Seth saw was not the ceiling but the stars. *What's going on?* he asked himself.

Seth looked around, trying to figure out just what might have happened. He and Max were on a dirt path in the middle of the woods. "Turn up the heat," his friend mumbled, rolling over.

"Get up," Seth commanded, rising to his feet.

"I'm tired. Your couch is *so* uncomfortable."

"Wake up Max."

"Why?" he questioned, opening his eyes slowly. When he saw stars, he quickly jumped to his feet. "Where are we?" Max looked this way and that, unable to believe what he was seeing. "Is this one of your jokes?"

There was no point in answering so Seth didn't. He knew nothing more than his friend.

After a moment or two Max suggested, "I think we should follow the path."

"No; that is not a good idea," replied Seth. "If we move around then it will be harder for people to find us."

Max grunted, but gave in. "Maybe we could build a fire... someone might see it."

Seth had to admit it was a good idea. The warmth would be nice. The leaves had not yet turned orange and red, but the night felt cold like fall. He was glad that he had slept in a long-sleeved shirt, unlike Max, who was wearing a tee-shirt. "Got your lighter?" Seth asked.

Max felt around in his jean's pockets and shook his head, "Must have left it in my jacket." Max stood up, hoping walking would bring some warmth to his body. "We could start a fire some other way."

"Got any suggestions?"

"Your always so proud of your Maine heritage. You used to say you knew everything about the woods."

"That's with proper camping gear," he replied, sitting down.

"Sure," the teen's tone had turned spiteful.

Seth's voice rose to match Max's, "Give me a break, Max! What do you want me to do—rub two sticks together?"

Max scowled. He said nothing more. Seth racked his brain—replaying watching the movie, falling asleep, and waking up here. He tried to find some logical reason why they might be in the middle of the woods, but no answers came to mind.

As the sun came up Seth grew restless and changed his mind, "I think you're right. We should move. If we follow the path it should lead us to something."

"Finally," exclaimed Max leaping up. Seth gave one more glance around him and they headed out. The teens followed the path closely. At some parts it got wider so that they could walk side by side, and at other points it was so small they could barely squeeze through one at a time. Seth always took the front.

As it grew to be mid-morning he began to regret wearing the long-sleeved shirt. The sun beat down upon them and he began to feel dehydrated. Seth knew that they would need to find water. From then on he kept eyes and ears open for any signs of a brook. "How did we get here?" Max questioned.

"I have no idea. I'm as lost as you," Seth answered and then stopped walking. "I think I hear running water." Following the sound, they went off the path, into the woods, and sure enough they found a little brook.

The boys drank their fill and went back to the dirt road. They traveled on for what seemed like hours and were soon very thirsty again, for the path had twisted farther and farther away from the water. Max and Seth were famished when they finally came to two houses mid-afternoon. The building to the left was made of wood; the one to the right was constructed of bundles of twigs. Seth knocked on the thick door of the hut to the right. "Oh, hello. Who are you?" inquired a jolly looking, human-sized frog, who was leaning on a steel cane and wearing a top hat.

Both boys stared at him. "I must be dreaming," exclaimed Max.

Rachel woke up in a soft, warm bed. The blankets were white and colorful pillows were all around her. She rolled over, slowly recovering her senses.

As Rachel looked around, she saw what you would expect to find in any normal bedroom—a dresser, a mirror, a closet, and some seating. *But the cloud wallpaper,* Rachel remarked to herself, *those clouds look so real.* Her eyes came to rest upon one thing that she did not expect to see. Wings.

They were neither like the feathers of angels nor the fragile wings of fairies, but looked more like the webbing on a ducks feet in a brilliant silver.

Rachel took a sharp breath. The woman standing in the doorway turned towards her, and seeing the shock on the teen's face, quickly retracted her wings.

"You're awake!" she exclaimed. As the woman got closer, Rachel could see how tall she really was, at least seven feet. She wore a flowing skirt and shirt. *What is this woman?* Rachel asked herself. "My name is Jennet and I am an airsprite. We live in the Enchanted Clouds, and that is where you are now," she told Rachel, as if in answer to her questions.

Airsprites! I remember imagining that there were tall ballerinas with wings who lived in the clouds and I called them airsprites, her mind raced. Rachel looked at the woman's feet and sure enough she was wearing ballerina shoes. *Now I know I'm dreaming!*

"Our queen passed away a week ago. Her daughter, Danielle, was the last surviving member of the Queen's family and so assumed the throne. Danielle made her first act as queen to send for you. With the help of Universe Girl, we found earth and brought you here."

Hearing the name 'Universe Girl', Rachel's mind was once again flood with memories. How many times as a small child had that character come into her stories? Rachel had loved to pretend that she was, in fact, Universe Girl. *The wallpaper must not be wallpaper at all,* she thought. *The clouds must be real!* Rachel closed her eyes. *When I look again,* she tried to convince herself, *I will not be seeing an airsprite standing on clouds.* She opened them. Everything was the same. *I'm certifiably insane!*

"It is a good thing we came to you when we did, for otherwise, you surely would have died," the woman told her.

"The twins!" Rachel exclaimed as memories of the fire filled her mind.

"Safe," Jennet quickly replied to calm her fears. "They are here as well. We didn't mean to bring them, but when we saw the two little girls, we could not leave them in the burning house to die." Rachel's brain was pounding. She now hoped all of this was real, for if it was not, she probably would not be waking up. Jennet continued, "The queen would like to see you as soon as you are able."

Rachel was silent for a few moments, letting everything that she had just heard and seen sink into her mind. *I'm in the clouds, with the airsprites. Universe Girl brought me here. A fire has burned down Mary and Elise's house. Now an airsprite queen wishes to talk to me. This is really, really weird...* "May I see the twins first?" she finally inquired.

"Of course. I will take you to them now." Rachel got out of bed, but as she tried to walk, dizziness overcame her. "Here, let me help you. You were in a burning building and that takes its toll on a person. You shouldn't expect to feel like yourself for a while."

Rachel looked around as they walked outside. The bright sun blinded her and she covered her eyes. Under Rachel's feet was a layer of cloud, and houses made of clouds were all around her.

Jennet pointed to the house next to them. "The girls are in there."

Rachel went inside, "Rachel!" yelled the twins as they rushed into her arms; her heart leaped to see those girls. "Look they have wings!" Mary exclaimed, pointing.

"And they're really, really nice. They love telling us stories and they have promised to take us flying!" Elise gleefully proclaimed.

Mary and Elise seemed well cared for. Rachel was confident enough to leave them. "That's great, girls. I have to go talk for a few minutes but I'll be right back. Be good."

"We will," they promised as Rachel walked out with Jennet.

Rachel told the airsprites, "Take me to the queen." She followed, her heart full of curiosity and disbelief. *How can what I imagined as a kid be happening around me? It is impossible!*

"Jennet...," Rachel began.

"Yes."

"Why does the queen want to see me?"

"I think I should let her answer that question."

Jennet led her to the biggest cloud building, one with a large rainbow overhead, and they walked in. Rachel guessed the dwelling was a palace, judging from its cloud pillars and throne, upon which sat a young woman wearing a rainbow crown. *Wow, this is cheesy,* Rachel decided. *My dreams are so weird!* "Your highness, this is Rachel Alexandra, the young woman you sent for," Jennet announced.

The lady, who was short for airsprites standards, rose from her throne and took Rachel by the hand. Her short brown hair and the freckles on her face made her look much too young to be a queen. "Miss Alexandra, thank you for coming. I will pass over the usual formalities and tell you right away why I called you here."

Chapter 3

"No, you're not dreaming," the frog declared, answering Seth and Max's astonished faces. It, excuse me, *he* was 5'8. A shirt made of colorful stones hung to his knees and he wore black pants. Seth and Max were surprised to see that the lean frog had only three fingers and toes on each hand and foot. "My name is Flibbert the frog. Who are you?"

Seth was now fully confident that he was dreaming, and figured it could do no harm to answer questions in a dream. "I am Seth Albert and this is Max...."

The frog interrupted with a gasp, "*You* are Seth! Come inside, quickly. Hurry, hurry." Flibbert was motioning with his hands and hopping up and down. He acted like whether or not they entered his house was life or death.

Both of the teens were about to go inside when a bulky minotaur came out of the hut across from the frog's. The creature was a couple of inches shorter than Flibbert, and was covered in dark fur. He had two horns coming off the top of his head and a black snout. The minotaur was more beast than man, but stood on two hooves. "Flibbert, you leave them to me. My master summoned Seth here. He is ours," he announced in a dark voice. It was then Seth noticed that the creature had an ax in his hand and wore a shirt of heavy armor.

Flibbert stood erect, his face stern and his body tense. "Now just one minute there, Samson," argued the frog bravely. "They don't have to go with you if they don't want to." Flibbert looked ready to fight, but what could a measly frog do against a strong minotaur?

Samson smiled, and Seth got a feeling that beneath the outward grin was a truly evil beast; however, he ignored this thought. Samson threw his head back and laughed, "Ah Flibbert, you have so much to learn. These humans can't resist coming with me. People like them always end up going to visit my master; and why shouldn't they want to? He will make them princes."

Seth's ears perked up as the word 'prince', but he heard a voice inside him—the voice of the Holy Spirit, the Counselor from God,—say, *Don't trust him.* Seth glanced again at the ax in the minotaur's hand and wondered if he would have any choice but to go with him. "Come on Seth, you and your buddy. Come through my house and I will take you my master." Max took several steps forward. Seth tried to pull him back. The minotaur got behind them and commanded, "Come along boys," pushing them with the wood of the ax.

"Now, you can't do that, Samson. You can't force them to go," Flibbert informed him.

"Boys, do you want to come meet a king and be treated as princes? Eat all that you want and be dressed in royal garb? And command hundreds and thousands of troops? If you don't, then I won't make you, but you will be passing up the opportunity of a lifetime." As he said, this he lowered the ax and stepped next to Max. "I'm in!" Max exclaimed.

Seth looked at Flibbert and felt squeamish—he wanted to go but he felt guilty because he knew better. "Who *is* your master?" he asked the minotaur.

"Smolden the dragon."

A picture came into Seth's mind of black creature over twelve feet tall. Covered in dark scales, it was fearsome beast.

When Seth had still lived in Maine, his pastor had read from the book of Job in the Bible about a leviathan. The boy's interest had instantly been sparked as the pastor described exactly what Seth thought a dragon should look like. The child had grabbed a piece of paper and a pencil and had sketched out the exact descriptions of the dragon, or as close as a six year old could come. He had named it

Smolden and shown the drawing to his friend Rachel. Together, they pretended that the dragon was the king of every bad guy they had ever faced in their imaginings. But Seth hadn't thought about the dragon in years. "Smolden," he murmured trying to draw up more memories. "Yes; you remember him. He remembers you too. That's why he called you here."

Now Seth really wanted to go with the minotaur. The thought of actually meeting a dragon, his own creation, thrilled Seth, even if it was only in a dream.

"I'll go," Max wholeheartedly answered.

"Don't," Flibbert's voice was barely audible.

Seth glanced at him. The frog face looked genuinely concerned. It was apparent to Seth that Flibbert was good and Samson was evil, but it was only a dream after all, and what fun would it be to choose to stay behind and not see the dragon? He nodded to the minatour to let him know that he would go. The three walked towards the door to his house. Flibbert watched helplessly from the sidelines. He could not stop them if they wanted to go—that just was not how things worked.

"Wait!" shouted a female voice from behind them.

Seth and Max turned around to see a girl about their age, coming out of Flibbert's house. Obviously Max had no idea who she was and Seth only slightly recognized her. "Rachel?" he asked, as her identity began to dawn on him. She had the same long, straight, light hair that she had always had; and the same slender figure; but it was her intense, brown eyes that were unmistakable.

His voice was all that was needed to trigger her memories. He looked much different than the last time she had seen him. His pudgy, childish figure had been replaced with a wiry frame, and he carried himself with the balance of an athlete. The dirty-blond hair and deep blue eyes, however, were the same. Rachel questioned, "Seth? What are you doing here?"

"You know her?" inquired Max, worried that the pretty girl would hinder Seth from going with the minatour. He understood his friend well enough to know that in general Seth chose to go with the flow, or in the direction of the most persuasive individual.

Rachel studied Seth's companion. He had a gangly form and kept his hands in his jean pockets. The freckles of a boy marked his face and his black hair was cut short.

Without looking at Max, Seth answered, "We were childhood friends." He was still staring at Rachel, not believing that she was standing in front of him. Talking frogs, live minatours, childhood friends—for the thousandth time that day, he reminded himself that he was definitely dreaming.

"Seth," Rachel rolled her eyes, "tell me you're not going with him."

"Well...I..." Seth bowed his head. When he looked up he was newly determined, "But not anymore. Come on Max, we are not going." He walked towards Rachel.

"Tell me you are not backing out just because of a girl," Max complained.

"No. I am not going because you and I both know that something is wrong here."

Max rolled his eyes. The minotaur snorted. Samson realized that there was no way Seth was going with him—at least not willingly. He put his ax into swinging position. "You *are* coming with me Seth," he told him. It was then that Max realized that Samson was no nice beast and started to run towards Seth and Rachel.

The minotaur launched himself at the teen, grabbing him around the knees and pulling him to the ground. Max let out a yelp before he got a face full of dirt.

Samson lumbered to his feet, hoping to get to Seth before Flibbert intervened, but the minotaur was slow and the frog was speedy. Flibbert jumped to where Samson stood. The minotaur swung his ax at the frog's head. Flibbert blocked easily with his steel cane. He then jumped up and kicked Samson in the chest, throwing the beast backward. Before Samson could regain his balance the frog was at his side, dealing him blow after blow with the cane, but it seemed to have little affect on the minotaur.

Samson used all his upper-body strength to swing at Flibbert's feet, but the agile frog jumped up just in time. Flibbert hopped backwards; Samson ran after him, but whenever the beast got close,

Flibbert jumped to a new position. "Too afraid to come near me, Frog?" Samson hollered, but Flibbert did not change his tactics in response to the enemy's taunts.

The frog leaped near Samson's house, but this time the beast did not run after him. Instead Samson thrust himself towards Seth, Rachel and Max. In two long jumps the frog stood in front of the teens. Samson snarled and readied his ax to swing again. He was breathing heavily, but he was sure that the battle would be over soon. If the frog hopped away, Samson would be able to grab Seth. If Flibbert did not move, the minatour would overpower him and kill him.

The frog's tongue shot out with lightning fast speed and hit Samson's right eye. The beast howled and fell backwards.

Flibbert instructed the three humans, "Get out of here!" They were hesitant to leave him, but his voice was stern and not to be questioned. They started to scurry away.

As Seth looked behind him, he saw Flibbert strike the minotaur in the snout. The beast growled in pain—Seth remembered imagining that minotaurs' noses are very sensitive. Samson attacked the frog in a rage, but Flibbert had the upper hand and a level head. His tongue shot out towards the other eye. It looked like Flibbert stood at least a chance of winning against the beast. Seth really hoped he did.

Chapter 4

"What could have happened to Flibbert?" asked Rachel as they hid behind some bushes waiting for the victor of the battle to come looking for them. They were far enough away from the frog and minatour's houses that they could not see them nor hear them, so they had no way of knowing what was happening.

"I don't know." Seth's answer was brief but not snappy. He was worried for the frog; he was wondering how it could be talking; and he was absorbed in thoughts of the past. He barely remembered Rachel; even though they had been friends for eight years, that was eight years ago.

"Why don't we move on?" asked Max. "Who cares about a stupid frog anyway?"

"He saved our lives!" Rachel exclaimed, shocked that Seth's companion would ask such a question.

"Whatever," Max replied sourly.

"Well, it is getting really dark. Let's go farther into the woods for better cover and get some sleep," Seth declared. Max's attitude was not helping his own. He wanted to go home, back to his air conditioner, shower and music, but unless he really was dreaming, home seemed awfully far off. He really had no clue why he thought they would be safe deeper into the woods, but somebody had to make decisions.

Even though Rachel could probably have found a good place to sleep much faster, she let Seth lead them away from the path and into the pucker brush of the woods. She smiled to herself, *At least if the boys are in front, I will know when to duck the snapping branches and how to avoid the prickly bushes.*

They finally settled down next to a broad stream—they were glad for the clean water. The mossy bed the three teens laid down upon was more comfortable than sleeping on the fallen branches by the edge of the woods, but it did not compare to their soft mattresses.

They laid on their backs and stared up at the stars. Seth liked constellations, but, living in the crowded city of New York, he seldom saw them. He had to admit that the thought of sleeping in the woods, under the night sky, not knowing where he was, was an appealing adventure. Still, he would much rather have been at home.

Rachel had a thousand questions for Seth, but began with the most pressing, "Who's your friend and how did you get here?"

Seth took a breath and started to tell what he knew, which was not much, "His name is Max and I am not sure. I am not even sure where here is, or if I am dreaming. The last thing I remember is falling asleep while Max and I were watching a movie in my parent's den. We woke up in the middle of the woods, and at first light followed a dirt path to where you met us. What is your story?"

And how conveniently he forgets just who's idea it was to follow the path, Max thought, though he remained silent. *If it hadn't have been for me he would still be sitting in the woods!*

"I was babysitting twin girls," Rachel began, hoping she could tell her tale clearly. She had a lot to say and knew more than Seth did, only because Queen Danielle had given her a brief overview of what was going on. "Lighting caused a fire in the house. I tried to get the girls' window open but couldn't. I passed out. When I woke up, I was with the airsprites."

"Wait. Airsprites?" Seth was puzzled by the name.

"Yeah, they have wings and live in the clouds. I met their queen and she told me that she was the one who ordered that I be brought here."

Rachel paused. What she was about to say confused her. How could she explain it to him? "Seth, you are going to think I am crazy, but you have to believe your eyes. Queen Danielle told me that everything you see here is built off of the stories we created as children

—the airsprites, Flibbert the frog, the minotaur, everything. Some things I created, some things you did, and some things we created together.

"There are two continents in this world. One they named Issym, which contains the things you created and the things you and I created *together*. The other they call Asandra and it is made up of just my creations. The whole world is called 'Xsardis' which literally means 'the ground beneath your feet.'

Rachel fidgeted. She hated to sound silly and knew that what she was saying seemed childish. She looked at Seth's face to see what he was thinking; but was he even listening? His eyes were locked on a nearby tree. Rachel remembered that as a child he always focused on some inanimate object when he was thinking. He must have been pondering what she had said, but what he thought of it, she could not tell.

Rachel decided to continue anyway. "The queen summoned me because Issym is falling apart. She told me that, just as we dreamed, the airsprites live in the clouds. Frogs, humans, and other creatures live on the surface. The minotaurs and other evil creatures (including some humans and toads—that is what they call frogs who serve evil) live beneath the ground, led by Smolden the dragon. There has long been a battle going on between the undergrounders, as Smolden's troops are called, who are on the side of darkness, and those on the side of light.

This chick is crazy, Max decided.

"The airsprites are vital in keeping Smolden underground. They didn't tell me why; they just said they were. Flibbert serves the airsprites by guarding the passage to their home and making sure that no one is forced beneath the ground. Apart from his diligent work, the undergrounders would have taken over the airsprites' domain, and then Smolden would have been able to come above ground. Samson the minotaur serves the evil ones, trying to convince people to go underneath and serving as the guard to the underground.

"The airsprites received news that the undergrounders are planning an attack. The continent of Issym needed help. They needed someone with a great knowledge of this world and the evil ones, so that they could defeat the undergrounders."

"And you're that someone?" Seth questioned.

"No, they thought I was, but I am not. Now I am on my way to find Universe Girl. She is the one who can send the twins and I home."

Seth had to laugh, *Universe girl? What a corny name!*

Rachel tried to ignore his snicker. "So, what do you think?"

"What do you mean?" Seth replied, turning his gaze from the tree to Rachel.

"Do you think I'm crazy? Do you think you're dreaming? Are you confused? Do you believe me? I mean, I only barely remember any of the stuff we imagined as kids and this all seems impossible, but I don't seem to be waking up..."

"Honestly?" Seth asked. Rachel nodded and he continued, "This all seems kind of far-fetched to me. Why would what *we* imagined become real?"

"I don't have an answer for you."

Rachel switched topics to keep the conversation from dying out. She wanted to keep Seth talking so she could figure him out. "Do you think Flibbert is all right? I mean, he's just a frog and that other guy was a huge minotaur."

Before he could answer, they heard movement in the water beside them. The three teens turned to find out what made the noise, and there stood Flibbert. He was carrying several fish in his left hand.

"Did you come from the water?" Seth asked.

"Yes."

"Wouldn't traveling by land have been easier?" Rachel inquired.

"After a tough battle, all a frog desires is a nice swim. Besides, I caught you some dinner," Flibbert grinned, as he began to build a cooking fire.

"*You* defeated the minatour, all by yourself?" Max questioned, intrigued that the seemingly powerless frog could even stand a chance against a strong beast like Samson.

"Actually, frogs are renowned all over Issym for their quick reflexes, which makes them great warriors."

By the light of the fire Rachel saw Flibbert's tired face and the wounds on his face and arms. They looked painful, but she thought that he would be fine after a good night's rest.

Seth saved his other questions until the fish had been cooked. "Where have you been?" he asked Flibbert.

"After I battled Samson, I tied him up and asked him a few questions. He told me that the undergrounders are planning an attack on the fairies near Kembar Plains, which is on the other side of the continent. I had heard rumors, but this is the first real proof we have. And Samson said we didn't have much time. Smolden will attack soon.

"Then, through an interesting series of events, Samson got away. I looked for him for quite sometime but when I didn't find him, I came here so that we could travel together."

Max did not want Flibbert to come with them. He had not liked the frog since he tried to stop them from going with the minotaur, even though the teen had discovered that Samson was evil. "Shouldn't you be back at your post?" he inquired, hoping that Flibbert would go away.

The frog shook his head, "No, I've got to warn the other frogs that the undergrounders are planning an attack."

"Flibbert," Seth started, "if you knew before about the attack, why didn't you warn them earlier?

He looked at Seth in the eye. "We talked about it, but didn't want to risk everything on a rumor. If we rally there, our towns and villages are vulnerable. Besides, what hope did we have before you and Rachel came? Frogs are brave, but the others, they were too scared to fight."

"Haven't you defeated Smolden before?" asked Rachel.

"Yes, but only with the gem of light. There are whispers all around the continent that he must have found a way not to be hurt by its light. The frogs don't believe it, but the others do.

"Now everybody, get some sleep. We've got much ahead of us." Soon Seth, Rachel, and Max were resting. Flibbert stayed awake all night, making sure that no one came close to the sleeping teens.

Sasha was not happy and someone was going to pay for her displeasure. She had had to leave her captives behind because someone had been following her. They, like her, were shape shifters—she was sure of it. Sasha had felt their presences and seen their slight movements. They had been tracking her ever since she got back from retrieving Seth and the person with him. Unwilling to lead them to her hideout, she had hidden the two in the woods and turned back to face her trackers. Of course they had run away before she could get to them. Cowards! But Sasha would not quit that easily. She knew who was responsible and he was going to suffer for the trouble he had caused.

But why would he do it? she pondered. Surely even if he had been dumb enough to work against her, he would not do so now that she had partnered with Smolden.

A long time ago, Smolden the dragon had stolen one of Universe Girl's magical orbs that allowed her to go to other worlds. Sasha had pilfered it from the dragon. In olden days, Smolden would have hunted down such a thief and destroyed her, but now, he was confined to the underground and he doubted that his entire army could have found, let alone killed, the shape shifter.

It was only a month ago that Sasha received a summons from Smolden. He had realized that her power could be put to work in his plan to recapture Issym. In exchange for certain services from Sasha, Smolden would allow her to co-rule Issym and he would teach her how to obtain eternal youth—one of the only abilities the powerful shifter had not gained. This was an offer she could not refuse.

One of the tasks that he required of her was that she would go to Earth using her orb and retrieve Seth, so that Smolden could question him and extract the knowledge he needed to take over the continent.

Arriving in New York City, New York, Sasha discovered how hard it would be to find someone in that crowded and foreign place. At least houses on Earth were easy to break into. Her bag was full of precious treasures they had had lying around—pills and perfumes and gold.

As far as Sasha was concerned, earth was far superior to Issym. With a press of a button, you could spy on other people's lives through something humans called a TV. Sound could be carried from house to house on what they had named phones. Inventions like that could revolutionize Xsardis. She felt her hands shake when she thought about equipping an entire army with Earth's devices, but that would have to wait.

It had been difficult, but Sasha had found Seth. Using one her herbal potions, she had put him and his friend to sleep. *I will bring them both. Perhaps the other will be of some use and if not I can always kill him,* the ruthless woman had thought. So she had brought both Seth and Max back to Issym, but made a change of plans. *If Smolden receives the boy, he will have no reason to keep his promises,* she had thought. *I shall take them to my hidden domain and then send word to the dragon.*

Sasha had proceeded to her home, but she had felt as if she were being watched. She had quickly realized that shape shifters were the cause of her trouble. Unwilling to be followed to her hidden lair or to take the teens to Smolden, Sasha had hidden them deep inside the woods.

She immediately headed for her brother, who ruled the shape shifters, deciding that he was the one responsible for the spies and outraged with him for interfering in her plan. *He will pay for this treachery,* she cursed. Sasha took on the form of a bear and charged in the direction of shape shifter territory.

Chapter 5

"Where is my prisoner?" hissed the black leviathan Smolden to an unfortunate human, who had brought the beast a cow for dinner.

The man, one of the undergrounders, cowered in fear before the giant beast and answered, "I don't know, my lord. The shape shifter woman should have returned with him long ago."

Smolden was in a foul mood. He hated every creature on Xsardis, but most of all, he hated the shape shifters. They thought they were high and mighty just because they could change forms. Idiots. They had no idea what true power was. With an inadequate battle plan they had once fought against the people of Issym. They lost, terribly, and were very near extinction before Sasha had come to power and led them to a new age. Of course, shape shifters never finish anything they start. Sasha had given control of the shifters to her brother so she could concentrate on other things. She had *given up* power!

Sasha. Smolden actually spit as he thought the name; the acid burned a whole in the floor. She had high aspirations, but that was the only kind thing the dragon could think of her.

Now Smolden had power. Scales that no forged weapon could break through; fire he could summon on command; powerful legs and claws; a wingspan of twenty feet; razor sharp teeth; horns coming out of his head; spikes running up his deep black back; and charisma that none could resist. When he spoke, men trembled. Whatever he sought after, he got. No human or frog or minatour or shape shifter had ever resisted him. He understood their weaknesses and that was his greatest strength. He knew Sasha's weaknesses, and that was why she would one day fall. She was an open book to him, easy to read, easy to comprehend. The thought of her frailty pleased him, but as he looked down at the human in front of him and recalled that Sasha had not yet brought Seth to him, he grew angry. Perhaps he had not seen into her as well as he had thought.

When Smolden had summoned Sasha, he had observed her carefully, in order to learn what she most desired. He quickly realized that she was power hungry. Money meant nothing. Power, everything. And she was the type of creature that would not settle for anything less than everything. It worked to his advantage. He knew that she would never share power, but neither would he; and her own lust for authority would drive her to great lengths. He could use a minion that would do anything, but one that could be dispatched when the time was right.

Sasha did not yet know her place. She constantly tormented him with memories of how he had lost power in Issym. And she loved to remind him that the mighty dragon needed *help* from her. Help. Smolden needed no one's help. From his powerful legs to the fire he loved to breathe, Smolden was deadly. He was all-powerful; he would never die. No one else could say that; and no one else ever would. The dragon would never keep his promises to Sasha.

It was true, though, that there were set backs to being as gargantuan as Smolden. He could never go unnoticed. He could never pretend to be something he wasn't. Sasha could become anything she wanted and go anywhere without being seen. What Smolden needed for domination, however, was not secrecy—it was Seth. He surely knew secrets of Issym and a way to release the dragon from his captivity in the underground. Smolden had realized that he would have to make an agreement with Sasha. Since she possessed the orb, she was the only one who could go to earth. So he had grudgingly made a deal with her. She could co-rule Issym if she helped Smolden capture the continent and he would teach her the secret to eternal youth. He did not actually know the secret. A leviathan never dies; it is his nature. There is no magic to it. As far as Smolden knew, he was the only dragon there ever was or ever would be. But Smolden was not concerned that he could not follow through on his end of the bargain. Deals were made to be broken. He would kill her when she had outlived her usefulness. He was beginning to wonder if she had already done so.

Sasha had not yet returned with Seth. Perhaps he had misjudged her. Maybe Sasha was wise enough to keep the boy as a bargaining chip to ensure her own safety. He cursed himself for the folly of trusting a shape shifter. They were naturally deceitful and he had let himself be duped by their leader!

Smolden would have taken his frustration out on the human in front of him had not a minotaur come into his presence. The beast bowed in front of the leviathan and did not raise his head until Smolden commanded, "Stand up."

The minotaur did not move and reported, "I am Samson, Lord Smolden. I guard the entrance to the Underground. The boy you sent for, Seth, and a friend of his came to my door."

"Was the shifter woman with them?" growled the dragon.

"No, my lord, it was just the two boys. I tried to force them to come to the underground but the airsprites' guard, a frog by the name of Flibbert, got in my way. The two boys and a girl ran off into the woods."

"You let them get away!" shouted the leviathan.

"My lord, please…" These were the last words uttered by Samson the minotaur. Smolden did not tolerate failures. In one bite, he swallowed the minotaur.

Smolden hissed one word in his fury, "Flibbert…."

"Wake up," Flibbert ordered, shaking Max. Max swatted the frog's hand and rolled over. "Come on, time to go. We've got to save all Issym, you know."

Once they got walking, Seth picked up with his questions again. "So Rachel, why couldn't the airsprites just send you home?"

"I'm not sure," Rachel replied.

"Well, they couldn't have taken you home unless they used one of Universe Girl's glowing orbs," Flibbert informed them.

"Orbs?" inquired Seth.

"Oh yes," answered the frog. "She has a universe in each of the spheres. They are clear and contain shining, white stars and milky constellations. You can actually put your finger through the orbs, though they look like glass. No one knows where she got them. With the orbs, all you have to do is touch a galaxy and then touch a planet, moon, or sun and you will be taken right there."

Rachel thought, *That is just what I imagined! I can't wait to see her and the orbs.*

"Those orbs are nothing compared to the original ball. It's said that it was the size of a building (though personally I think that is an exaggeration). You could actually step inside the orb and touch a solar system. Once you touched the solar system, its galaxies would expand. Then you could touch a galaxy and the ball would fill up with all its planets, moons, suns, asteroids and anything else in space."

Max commented, "That's no different than the smaller orbs."

Flibbert continued, "If you'll let me finish I'll explain the difference. When you touched the master ball and picked a planet, for example, you could pick a continent, a closer location, a house, and finally a person. When you touched the person you would be rushed right to them. The smaller orbs would only take you to a planet."

"Flibbert, that's amazing!" Rachel exclaimed.

Seth was curious, "So where is this master ball?"

Flibbert replied, "No one really knows. It just disappeared."

"Yeah right! More likely it never existed," Max said quietly.

As they traveled, Seth tried to draw Max into the conversation, but every time the teen simply gave a curt reply and turned his head. After a while Seth gave up, and just enjoyed the company of Rachel and Flibbert.

They walked until they came to a village. In it, they could see about a dozen wooden and twig huts. Some of them were built on the ground, and some were up on stilts. Frogs moved about, doing their daily duties.

A male frog dressed in the same kind of shirt that Flibbert wore, and carrying a sword on his belt, came out of the house at the far end of the village. A female frog wearing a dress followed him. Two smaller frogs, wearing miniature versions of the armor and swords their elders wore, came behind them. The first frog called out in a cheerful voice, "Flibbert!"

Flibbert embraced him, "Who else could it be?" He hugged the female, "How are you Maria?" He squeezed the two smaller frogs, "Have you been behaving, boys?"

They answered, "We have, Uncle Flibbert. Did you get any more bad guys?"

Flibbert smiled. "I sure did. Look at you, all dressed up in armor and wearing swords."

The little frogs' faces shone with pride. "Uncle Flibbert, these are the swords you gave us. Look."

"So they are." Flibbert admired their stone shirts, "And who made you such fine armor?"

"I did," answered Maria, putting her hand on the head of the older child.

"Should have known," answered Flibbert, "you're one of the best armor makers I've ever had the pleasure of being related to. You see my armor, boys? Your mom made this and I'll never replace it."

Flibbert looked at his brother and tilted his head toward the two teens closest to him. "Finrod, this is Seth, and this is Rachel."

Finrod's eyes widened, "*The* Seth and Rachel?"

Flibbert nodded, "And this is Max, Seth's friend." Turning toward the teens, he said proudly, "Meet my twin brother Prince Finrod, and his wife, Princess Maria. These are their two boys, Azmaveth and Padon."

"Won't you please come in?" Finrod gestured toward the hut behind him.

Maria, Finrod, Flibbert, and Rachel entered the house. Seth was about to go in as well when Max shoved his way past him into the hut. "What was that for?" asked Seth, indignant.

Max did not answer. He simply continued into the house. As they sat down around a table, Seth whispered to Max, "I can tell that you've been angry with me all day! What's up?"

"Like you don't know," Max retorted.

"Actually, I don't," Seth replied. Their quarrel was interrupted when Flibbert began to say grace. When he was finished, Maria set a few loaves of bread on the table. Both Seth and Max forgot about the fight so that they could stuff their mouths. Maria quickly provided drinks, and then some chicken. The food was soon devoured.

"My brother, you look as if you haven't slept in quite some time," Finrod remarked.

"Last night wasn't the first night I was deprived of my sleep," Flibbert answered solemnly. "The undergrounders have been acting strangely. Someone always has to be awake and on guard. The airsprites have been helping me keep watch, but my hours of rest have been short and inconsistent. But enough about me. You probably want to hear about how I met Seth and Rachel."

Finrod and Maria hung on every word of Flibbert's story, eager to find out all they could about Seth and Rachel, the imaginers of their world. But Seth, Rachel and Max were impatiently waiting for the conversation to move onto other things. They had lived the tale that was being told; they had no interest in hearing it. Seth and Rachel felt awkward being treated like legends.

When Flibbert started to talk about what he had learned from Samson the minatour their ears perked up. "I instructed the three teens to run and stayed behind 'till I had beaten Samson. He confirmed that the undergrounders are planning to assemble at Kembar Plains. I'm sure that Smolden has chosen the fairies as his first target. If he overcomes them, Issym will have no hope." A realization came to the frog and his heart filled with fear, "Oh, Finrod, you and your village need to evacuate."

"Why?" Finrod questioned.

"Samson will go back to Smolden and tell him that I protected Seth and Max. The dragon will want Seth back with every inch of his evil body. He knows that you are my brother and that the first stop I would make would be here. Smolden will send his army to your village to retrieve Seth."

Finrod shook his head, "No, brother, we could never get out of here in time. We have many old frogs in this village. We also have many trained warriors, who will fight."

"You won't be able to defeat Smolden's troops. He will send too many," Flibbert protested.

Finrod held on to hope. Looking at Seth and Rachel he asked, "Could either of you tell us anything that would help us defeat Smolden?"

Rachel replied, "Don't look at me. Seth created him."

"Who? Me?" Seth replied.

"Don't be alarmed, though. In all games there has to be a bad guy. You probably just created Smolden to be the villain in one of your stories. Do you remember the time we locked the princess—that was me—in the tower and an evil dragon guarded it? We didn't realize the creatures we imagined were going to become real.

"The airsprites thought I might have created Smolden, but I never pretended that there was a dragon in my stories. You must have imagined him. Do you remember any of his weaknesses?"

All eyes were on Seth, whose own eyes were on Max, as he answered Rachel, "I don't remember these creatures and I don't remember anything we played as kids. I tried to block all that out of my mind. Those were childish days that are now behind me. I don't want to go back and relive them. I wasted time imaging those silly things. It is of no value to me now."

Rachel stood up and looked Seth right in the eye. "Well it is of value to these people and of value to me. We created Issym. Flibbert and the airsprites are only alive because of us! You're saying that was wasted time? And if it is true that you wanted to forget about me, then I won't force you to look at me any longer!" She tore out of the house.

Seth looked at Max. He had a snobby smile on his face—his eyes were saying, "Good job. It's time you told that girl what for!" Seth avoided the others' faces. He knew they would not approve of what he had said.

Why had he said it, anyway? *Max had been mad at me, and now we're friends again. What's the problem?* He tried to justify himself, but he had an uncomfortable feeling in his heart. *No. I always say stupid, hurtful things like that. It's my fault. I've got to stop talking like that! I guess I'm going to need to apologize to Rachel...*

Flibbert continued, "Well, it would have been nice to have Seth and Rachel's help, but we've defeated Smolden before, we can do it again."

"Do not forget, brother," Finrod declared, "how much younger and more foolish the dragon was. He had a small army then and his power was limited. It is not so now."

"Then we need to get everyone together, more than just frogs, if we are going to have a prayer of helping the fairies. Rachel and Seth were planning on going to find Universe Girl, so she could send them home. I will go with them, and anyone I see I will inform of the coming battle. After that, I'll go to the other villages and tell them. Hopefully they will join our cause so that we can head to Kembar Plains to protect the fairies."

"Where shall we tell the villages to gather?" Maria asked.

"Prince Aldair's castle," Flibbert suggested.

"The human prince?" Maria questioned.

"Yes," Flibbert told them. "Since he lives a little more than half-way between here and Kembar plains, it will be the perfect meeting place."

Finrod agreed, "Aldair's castle it is."

"But your village really does need to evacuate," Flibbert urged.

"All right. I'll tell my people to start packing." Finrod sighed deeply, then stood up, with a hand on his sword.

"But they must be quick."

Max sat in the meeting, listening with only half his brain. A plan was forming in his mind and he thought it just might work.

Sasha arrived at the home of her brother. He was talking with three other shape shifters, but on seeing the venomous eyes of his sister, he quickly dismissed the others and went over to Sasha, cautious of her foul mood. "Sister," he greeted, trying to act casually, but fully aware of her strong powers and evil nature.

Her wicked eyes showed no mercy. "Edmund! You sent shifters to spy on me, didn't you!" she charged.

"What do you take me for? An idiot? I would never, ever spy on you," he pleaded.

"I felt shifter presences and they were following me. Do you call me a liar?"

"Of course not, Sasha," he trembled. "I'm sure shifters were following you if you say so, but they were not sent by me."

"Then who are they?" she shouted. "Do you not rule over all the shifters but me? Should you not be able to keep them all in check? When I surrendered control of the shape shifters to you so that I could focus on gaining more power, I assumed you would not fail me."

"A week ago a few rebel shifters left us," he cringed.

"Left? Who would dare disobey you, who have my authority to rule? Who is their leader?" she questioned. Edmund stared at the ground and did not answer. "Who!" Sasha thundered.

"Kate," he answered, quietly.

"Ah...Kate." Sasha recognized the name and her tone changed. "You would not go after the woman you love," she mused, and then her voice grew menacing again. "And now I have been delayed by your weakness!"

"Sister," Edmund answered rapidly, "it is not any emotion that keeps me from going after her. We simply don't know where Kate and her rebels are."

"Why not? You should be able to find them."

"You don't understand. Kate is more powerful than other shifters. She knows things and can do things that normal shape shifters don't and can't. It will be almost impossible to track her down."

"Is she superior in skill to you, brother?" Sasha questioned harshly.

"Perhaps," Edmund whispered.

Sasha was surprised at his answer. She and her brother were descended from an ancient line of shape shifter kings and, therefore, should have been the most powerful of shifters. If Kate really was more powerful than Edmund, then she too, must have some kind of royal lineage and could possibly contend for rule of the shifters. *This is not good,* thought Sasha. *If Kate assumes control, she may not be as compliant as Edmund.* She had no concern for her brother, only for what was better for her.

"Does she serve Smolden?" Sasha asked, trying to determine the damage Kate could do.

Edmund shuffled his feet and answered, "No."

Sasha leaned in close to her brother and put a cruel hand on his shoulder. When he felt how firmly she gripped him, he realized that if he ever failed her again he would not live to see another day.

Edmund had not lifted his head since the conversation had turned to Kate. Sasha put one slender finger, the nail sharpened to a point, under his chin and lifted up so that their eyes met. "You will find Kate and the rest of those with her and bring them back here, where they will be appropriately punished. You will do it soon. You would do well not to fail me again," she ordered sharply. Sasha would have told Edmund to kill Kate, but it is almost impossible to kill a shape shifter—it can only be done under unique circumstances.

If Kate is really as powerful as Edmund says and she was the one on my trail, she could have easily woken my captives. I must get back to where I left Seth and the other boy! she thought. Sasha took on the form of a hawk, heading for the spot she had left the sleeping Seth and Max, but they were already long gone.

Chapter 6

When the meeting finally ended, Flibbert went to find Rachel. He discovered her behind Finrod's house. "Rachel, I'm sorry about Seth."

She answered, "No one said he had to like me. But last night and this morning when we were talking, it was like we were friends, and I was sure that he could at least tolerate me. With what he just said, though, I guess I was wrong."

"I don't think he meant it. That doesn't make it much better, I know. Would you do me a favor? Give him a second chance. He did look really thoughtful after you left. Maybe he's sorry. Be the better person. Forgive."

Rachel bit down on her tongue, something she did frequently to keep herself from answering too quickly. It helped her to avoid saying things she would regret. "Okay, Flibbert. I'll try, but it's going to be hard."

"Good girl. I know there's a lot going on, but as the Bible says, 'a kingdom divided against itself will be ruined and a house divided against itself will fall.' If you two are not working together, things are going to be much harder for you.

"Now, tell me. I think Seth and Max still have doubts that Xsardis is real. What about you—do you have doubts?"

Rachel took a breath and answered, "No. This is all happening. I don't know how, but it's happening."

She stood up and went back into Finrod's house. Maria was the only one left in the hut. She was doing the dishes. "Can I help you with that?" Rachel offered, wanting to get her mind off Seth's cruel words.

"Sure," the frog woman replied. "Thank you very much." Maria informed Rachel of everything that had been said in the meeting after she had left. "There's much to be done to pack up the village and very little time."

Rachel helped Maria until to put her household in order until it was dinnertime. Then the women emerged from the house, into the hustle and the bustle of the village. Seeing the frog's piling their possessions into carts, Maria went over to her husband and had a hushed conversation with him. "There's no way that we'll make it out of the village with all this stuff," she told him. By *we* she meant the whole village. "If we go with nothing but a pack on our backs we might outdistance the army."

"I know, darling," her husband replied, taking her hand in his. "But what choice do we have? Our whole lives have been here."

"We won't have our lives if we stay here much longer," she respectfully informed him.

Meanwhile, Seth had gotten up his courage and gone over to talk to Rachel. "I'm a jerk and I'm sorry," he said.

Rachel sighed, "It's alright. We all make mistakes."

Seth could tell her heart was not in accepting the apology. "When I moved to New York everything was different and I took on a new way of life. I stopped imagining and started trying to please people, whatever it took, even hurting other people. Max is my best friend and he was mad at me. By wounding you, I could please him. But that's no excuse and I'm really sorry."

Rachel smiled. She truly forgave him, "Let's put it behind us."

Fish caught in the nearby river, as well as a collection of fruits, were being served for dinner. Everyone was seated around a fire, keeping warm. Everyone—that is, except those watching for any signs of the enemy undergrounders approaching.

Seth and Rachel sat down on a log beside Azmaveth, Finrod's firstborn, to eat. "I love fish. Don't you?" the frog child asked.

"I never liked the fish in my world but here I think they taste really good," answered Rachel.

"How old are you Azmaveth?" Seth inquired.

"I'm nine and a half, sir."

"Why do you call me *sir*?" questioned Seth.

"You're a knight, right? If a frog's a knight we call him sir. So I figured that since you're a knight I should call *you* sir."

"They have probably heard about all the times you rescued me from towers or fought off dragons. Our stories must be legends here," Rachel laughed.

"Yes fair lady," responded Azmaveth. "My favorite story is about the time you and Seth climbed Mt. Smolden to find the gem of light. You had to fight countless foes but you still made it up. When I heard that story, I knew I wanted to be just like you, Sir Seth."

"I don't remember that," Rachel declared.

Seth smiled, "I do."

Rachel asked, "Would you tell me?"

"Oh yes, please tell us," pleaded Azmaveth.

"You said it was your favorite story. Surely you've heard it before," Seth shrugged.

"Yes, but never from you." The frog child looked expectantly at Seth.

"Well, I'll try," he told them. "Smolden the dragon and his army had been attacking frog and human villages as well as the mushnicks." (Mushnicks are three feet tall, and their faces can be blue, white, orange, or other colors. Their baggy clothes are as colorful as their faces and they are extremely cheerful. They serve the fairies and the fairies care for them, treating them like little children, for they certainly act like it. Though childlike, the mushnicks surpass all in good character and more noble beings cannot be found.) "So the mushnicks, the humans and the frogs got together and discussed what to do. The frogs and humans sent their fiercest warriors to fight, and the mushnicks equipped them with all kinds of armor and weapons (as well as sending a few of their own people to battle), but the dragon killed those brave soldiers.

"The mushnicks went before the fairy Elaine and asked her what to do. She told them, 'Climb Smolden's mountain and find the gem of light. Smolden is hiding it so that no one will be able to use it against him, for he hates its light; it can kill him if he is exposed to it for too long. If you bring the gem back to me, I will set it up so it burns bright and protects the ground from him. He will be forced beneath the surface of Xsardis.

"'But who?' they asked, 'Who shall go?'

"'The two children I am sending you shall go,' she replied."

"Seth," interrupted Max as he walked over, waking the two humans and the frog from their absorption in the story, "I need to talk to you."

"I'll finish later," Seth promised Azmaveth and Rachel, getting up. "What is it?"

Max led Seth over to where Flibbert stood. "So what is this all about?" Flibbert questioned with impatience; Max's bad attitude had not escaped the frog's notice.

"I have an idea of how to give you an advantage over Smolden," Max declared.

"What do you mean?" Flibbert inquired, curious in spite of himself.

"When we first got here, Samson the minotaur offered Seth and I positions as princes in the underground."

"Correct, but we declined," Seth put in.

"I think Smolden will let us reconsider," Max replied.

"But we are not going to," Seth told him firmly.

"Yes we are, because we are going to be spies. We can find out what he is planning. Also, if we go to Smolden, the frog village won't be in danger any more, right? The undergrounders would only come here to get us; if we are with Smolden, than this village will be safe."

Flibbert and Seth actually considered the plan—for about three seconds. "Not a good idea," Seth responded.

"Certainly not," Flibbert agreed.

"Why not?" questioned Max. The teen had no real interest in helping Issym; in fact, he would rather have helped Smolden, if the dragon would give him riches as a reward. If he could only reach him...

"Because it is far too risky," Flibbert informed Max. "The evil ones won't just reveal their plans to you and they certainly don't want to make you princes. They want to find out what you know about this world and then you will be of no use to them. No, it is definitely not a good plan."

Max still held on to hope. First Rachel had stopped them from going to the underground and now Flibbert was. He had to convince Seth to break away from these silly creatures and go with him to Smolden. "Seth, come on, don't listen to this frog. We could princes. Maybe they could even send us home."

It was tempting, Seth had to admit, but by now he was smarter than to agree. He knew that bad choices always looked good—until you made them. "No. Flibbert's right," Seth decided once and for all. Max turned and stormed off.

Flibbert sighed, "I worry about him."

"As do I," Seth replied. "Flibbert, I'm sorry about what I said in the meeting. I really want to help you and your people. I'm trying to remember anything, but it's so hard. I never thought that all this would be real. I never thought I would need to remember any of this stuff."

"So you believe that this isn't a dream?"

"I'm not convinced, but maybe. It certainly seems real. What about your village? Should Rachel, Max and I leave to keep you safe?"

Finrod approached, "Most definitely not. Everyone in my village would give their lives to protect you."

Why would they do that? Seth wondered.

Finrod handed Flibbert and Seth cups full of some sweet drink. "To success on your journey," he toasted. "Though I fear that you, Seth, may find that you must drop your own quest in favor of another."

"Why would you say that?" the teen inquired as he sipped his drink.

Finrod never answered this question, for the call rang out, "Intruders!"

Chapter 7

Rachel was startled by the shout, "Intruders!" Frogs jumped to their feet and began hurrying to gather their children or hop to their posts. Rachel told Padon, who had recently sat down with her, and Azmaveth, "Follow me," and led them towards their house.

Finrod was bellowing out instructions. "All warrior frogs prepare for battle. Archers to your positions! All those not involved with the fighting—leave the village and head to Prince Aldair's castle." As Finrod drew his sword, he told Seth, "Get Rachel and my kids and go to my house. Max too, if you see him. Maria will meet you there." He went back to shouting out orders.

Seth watched Finrod's determination, leadership and courage as he readied himself and his village for the coming battle. *And they are only in danger because they sheltered us!* Seth's admiration for the frogs of Issym was growing.

Seth hurried to Rachel's side. "Inside Finrod's house, all of you. Hurry!" he commanded.

"But I want to fight," Azmaveth protested.

Flibbert hopped down from a tree, from which he had been looking over the enemy. "How many of them?" Finrod asked.

"At least two hundred," answered Flibbert. "I never imagined Smolden would attack this quickly."

"I told Seth to gather my kids, Max, and Rachel inside the house," Finrod informed his brother. "Go to them and make sure they get out of here safely."

"There is no way I am leaving my brother to fight a war he can't win, while I run away and hide," Flibbert countered. "Especially when I brought that war to him."

"This isn't your fault, but Flibbert, you have to go."

"You have two children and a wife. Take them and leave. I have no family and I am just as competent to lead your frogs."

"No. This is my village. It is my duty." Finrod's face was stern.

"I'm no coward. Besides I grew up here, and that makes it my village too."

"I have responsibility for it. How could I leave my frogs? Would you have me be the coward?"

"We were twins, remember? The oldest child takes leadership of the village. I'm older." Flibbert was grasping at straws now.

"But you gave the village to me."

"Only because you wanted it," retorted Flibbert.

"You wanted to be a warrior!"

"Gentlefrogs!" shouted Maria, interrupting their fight. "We don't have time for this discussion. One of you quickly come with me. The other stay here and lead the troops. Or both of you come or both of you stay, but we need to go!"

Finrod answered, "She's right."

"I know she is," responded Flibbert, all too aware of what was coming.

"As the prince of this village…" Finrod started.

"Don't do this. You have a family."

"I command you to go."

Every frog is bound to obey their leader's orders; Flibbert had no choice but to do as he was told. "All right, brother. I'll go. Come, Maria, we've got to get you out of here."

Finrod pulled his wife close for one long second. Then, shouting a battle cry, he ran straight for the enemy that had now entered the village. Grabbing Maria by her three-fingered hand, Flibbert headed for his brother's house. "Come on kids, we've got to go," he ordered as he entered his brother's hut.

Maria hid her worry for her husband and the village from her children. She, with a face untouched by emotion, pulled open a hatch in the floor and pulled out weapons, which she distributed to those around her. "Why do we need these? Aren't we supposed to be heading away from the battle?" Max questioned.

"That army," Flibbert pointed his sword towards the door, "is here to find *you.*" Emotion rumbled through the frog's voice. "They won't stop after they destroy this village. They will keep hunting you." No one else said anything as they rushed to strap the swords on themselves and then hastened out the back door into the woods.

They moved quickly for an hour. Flibbert carried Azmaveth when the frog boy grew tired, and Seth picked up Padon. All would have shouted with joy when Flibbert said, "We'll rest here for the night," but they were too tired and out of breath.

Rachel felt unnaturally exhausted. She figured it was just her asthma but it seemed to be worse than normal.

"I'll take the first watch," Flibbert informed the group. "Seth, you're next; I'll wake you up in a while."

As Rachel stretched out, she heard Flibbert and Maria talking. "What road do you think the other frogs will take?" Flibbert asked Maria.

"I saw some of them running towards the river. They'll probably swim most of the way to Aldair's castle. We can only pray that the undergrounders won't follow them."

The teens and grown frogs took turns keeping watch, in case any undergrounders had followed their group. When morning came, Padon exclaimed, "I'm hungry."

"Hungry, lad?" came a response from the trees. "So are we."

Sasha descended from the sky and shifted from the form of a hawk to her preferred human form. She assumed the shape shifter Kate had already taken Seth and his friend, but she searched through the wooded area where had left them, just in case. As expected, they were gone. Sasha set her jaw and headed to the underground. She did not cherish the thought of informing Smolden that she had lost his prisoner.

Kate the shape shifter had a band of sixteen other shifters with her. These seventeen had broken away from Edmund, unwilling to serve either Sasha or Smolden. They did not want Issym to be taken over by evil.

Kate had led the 'rebel' shifters as they had tracked down Sasha. They watched silently as she hid her two captives and once she had gone, Kate had woken the prisoners. Then she led the rebels west. When she figured they were safe from Sasha, they stopped and spent many days discussing what should be done.

"We should go to the frogs," suggested one.

"No, they'll never believe we want to help," replied another.

"Well, if we aren't going to help the good guys what was the point of breaking away from Edmund?" still another questioned. "We've got to do what is right!"

"We already helped them enough. It's time we looked after ourselves," one shifter declared.

"We can't be selfish. We must help Issym."

"It is way too dangerous. If the frogs don't believe us, they have the power to kill us."

Much more discussion followed. For a long time Kate refused to give her opinion, afraid of becoming a dictator. She hated the thought that she had led the shifters away from one harsh ruler only to become one herself. But when she could stand their squabbling no more, Kate finally cut in, "There is a hope that Universe Girl will believe us. She does not judge by a person's appearance, but by his heart. If we win her approval, then we win all frogs' and humans' approval." No one disagreed. "We will go to her castle."

Chapter 8

As a voice from the trees rang out, "Hungry, lad? So are we," immediately seven men surrounded the band of humans and frogs. Two of the men were carrying bows and the other five were wielding swords. "Give us all your gold, jewelry, armor, and weapons," the leader commanded, pointing his blade at Flibbert.

Flibbert boldly told them, "We carry no gold and you will not have our weapons. You will have to kill me to take anything from our group."

"Perhaps you do not know who I am," the leader boasted. "I am Philip and these are my comrades. We travel around Issym robbing small bands of people like you and have yet to be defeated. We do not want to hurt noble frogs and humans such as yourselves, but we need to eat, and your jewelry and armor will buy us food for many weeks."

Flibbert slowly drew his sword, as if deciding whether to resist or surrender. Suddenly, he jumped forward off his powerful legs and attacked the leader. Seth drew his own weapon, as did those around him. *If these bandits really are skilled fighters,* thought Seth, *do we stand any chance of defeating them?*

Maria hopped towards an archer, who had pointed his bow at one of her children. She broke his weapon, but not before the man had got off a shot. The arrow lodged in her shoulder; Maria crumpled to her knees.

Rachel was working on disarming the other archer. That left four men to Seth, Azmaveth and Padon. Seth tried to keep an eye on the frog children as he launched himself at one of the bandits. His sword flashed up to meet his attacker's. Seth continued to parry. He would have thought that a master-swordsman could have disarmed him much more quickly.

Flibbert expertly wielded his sword against Philip; there was no question who was the better warrior. Rachel was now fighting one of the other bandits. Maria had not moved. Padon was at her side. Azmaveth gave up the battle and joined him. Where was Max?

In all the confusion Seth could not tell if they were winning. Rachel was holding her own, but she seemed to be moving slowly. She must have been getting tired. He feared they would be forced to surrender. Seth whispered a prayer under his breath.

The archers, whose bows were broken, had already disappeared. Rachel and Seth, though tiring, somehow managed to send two of Philip's band to the ground. Flibbert just kept bounding from one place to another and swinging his sword with all the strength he possessed. Seth could see that Philip was growing tired from trying to keep up with the frog.

Seth felt a sword scrape across his arm and saw the blood seeping from the wound. He was filled with anger—these bandits attacked them only for the sake of money. People were going to die over money! At least the men had enough chivalry to leave the frog children alone.

Seth heard Philip call out, "Halt, you win!" Had they won?

The three remaining bandits stepped together. Seth kept his eyes—and his sword—on them.

Rachel dropped to the ground, taking in great gulps of air. Her hands trembled with exhaustion. Flibbert sprung to Maria's side, examining her wound. He questioned Philip, "Do you have medicines?"

"No," he answered.

"Food?"

"No."

"You said you had never been defeated. Certainly you have some spoils left."

"I lied. We rarely win a battle. And we ate the last of our food yesterday." That made a lot more sense to Seth and Rachel than did their story about never having been defeated.

"How badly does it hurt?" Flibbert inquired of Maria, taking her hand.

"I'll be fine," she responded, attempting a smile.

"How far are we from the next frog village?" asked Seth urgently. He could see Maria's face growing pale and knew that she did not have much time.

"Three hours on foot," Flibbert told them. They heard the neighing of a horse.

"What was that? You said that you didn't have anything. Is that your horse?" Rachel questioned Philip.

"We have seven."

Flibbert rose and drew his sword. "No time for games," he declared, "This lady frog is dying. We need those horses."

"You can have them, but if you let me come along I can show you a shortcut that will get you there in half the time." Flibbert agreed. "Lead me to the animals."

While Flibbert and Philip went to retrieve the horses, Seth and Rachel stood guard. The two bandits still conscious took their weapons and started to move away. The teens made no effort to stop them. When the men on the ground woke, they also headed deeper into the woods. An eerie quietness came over the forest. Only the chirping of birds and the occasional sob from Padon could be heard. Rachel took a seat beside the frog child and put his head in her lap, trying to comfort him. "Everything's going to be alright. There is no one tougher than your mother," she told him.

A few minutes later, Philip and Flibbert returned. "Seth, where's Max?" the frog asked, noticing for the first time that the teen was missing.

Philip informed them, "That other boy you were with? The coward ran off at the start of the battle."

Idiot, thought Seth. *What am I supposed to do now? How am I expected to find him?*

The group of frogs and humans quickly mounted the horses and hurried to the nearest frog village. Philip's shortcut proved to be invaluable. When Flibbert saw the first signs of the town, he took off as fast as he could, getting there with Maria well before the rest of them. "This is the Princess Maria. Her husband is Prince Finrod. I am his brother Flibbert. She is in need of medical help," he called. Immediately frogs rushed out and carried her to the medical hut. The prince of the village, dressed in stone armor, sped towards Flibbert. "I am Prince Paseah. We know of your deeds, Flibbert the frog. You are welcome in this village." When he saw the humans ride in his face went pale. He shouted, "Intruders!"

Flibbert drew his sword, thinking that the prince was talking about undergrounders, and turned around. Then he realized that Paseah had spoken of Rachel and Seth and Philip. "No! They're friends!" he shouted quickly.

Prince Paseah looked at him inquisitively but he signaled his warriors to wait. Flibbert continued, "Two of them are Rachel and Seth, the ones who imagined our world. The frogs are the sons of the Princess Maria and the man is Philip—his is a long story," Flibbert explained.

"Let them be," shouted the prince to his subjects. "They are guests." Turning to Flibbert, he declared, "I will trust your word. What has happened to the Princess Maria?"

"She's near death from a wound she received in battle," Flibbert replied.

"She'll receive our best care," Prince Paseah assured.

"May I have a word with you in private?"

Paseah nodded. They stepped inside his hut and Flibbert told him, "Smolden is going to try to take back Issym. He is rallying all his troops at Kembar Plains. My quest is to get support from the villages and raise an army at Prince Aldair's castle. We must not let the dragon take Issym again."

"But how will he take Issym? He cannot leave the underground." It was not hard for Paseah to believe Smolden would try to conquer Issym again, but it was difficult to understand how the dragon would succeed.

"I don't know how, but if he's readying his army, he must have a plan. We need to be prepared."

Paseah knew how deadly it would be if Smolden really did come aboveground. "You have our support."

"Good. Send all your warriors to Prince Aldair's castle. He doesn't know that we are assembling there but I am sure he will not mind. He is a good man and will support our cause. Just let him know that I have sent you."

Rachel was not feeling well. Even riding a horse seemed to take a lot out of her. She sat down near Seth to rest and get back her breath. Seth started to tell Azmaveth and Padon more of the story he had begun in their village. Rachel admired him for trying to keep the kids' minds off their mother's wound and the fact that their father was probably dead. Philip was sitting nearby, but Rachel tried to ignore him. He was responsible for what had happened to Princess Maria.

"As you probably guessed," Seth began. "Rachel and I were the children whom the fairy Elaine had spoken of. We started our climb up Mt. Smolden with a bag full of provisions and water. I brought a sword and Rachel carried a dagger, as well as a specially crafted bow made of ivory and a quiver of arrows made of Smolden's shed scales.

"We hadn't even been five minutes on the mountain when we encountered our first band of enemies. They were the guards of Mt. Smolden, making sure that only those who were bad guys used the hill. Evil men made the mount their home and paid an entrance fee to use it. They went there to hide from the good guys or for other reasons, but anyway, Mt. Smolden was infested with villains. The higher you climbed, the fiercer the enemies got."

"These guards looked us over and asked what business we had on the mountain. I told them that our business was none of theirs. We tossed them a few gold coins and they let us pass.

"As we traveled, we saw many groups of thieves but none of them bothered us. They could tell that we weren't to be trifled with.

"We sat down and had lunch. I whispered to Rachel, 'Take this rock and pretend that you are sharpening your dagger. We need to play the part of dangerous criminals.' She did so and it discouraged anyone from bothering us."

Flibbert came over and informed the group, "Maria is going to be just fine. At this point, she simply needs rest. Boys, you can go see her now." They jumped to their feet with lightning fast speed. Nothing would keep them from rushing to their mother's side.

"Tomorrow," Flibbert told Rachel and Seth, "I'll go with you and see that you get to Universe Girl. It isn't safe for you to travel alone. Then I'll continue trying to raise an army. Are you sure you won't stay and help us?"

Seth declared, "We just want to go home."

"We can't really help you anyway," Rachel added, trying to justify Seth's answer so it did not sound so selfish.

Home seemed so far off. Even if Universe Girl could help them, they would have to retrace their steps and find Max. Then they would need to retrieve Mary and Elise from the airsprites. Being the people most desired by Smolden, all that would have to be done while dodging undergrounders.

Back at the Finrod's village, the women, children, and older frogs escaped. Some of the warriors got away, but most of them were slaughtered, including the great Finrod, who defeated more of the undergrounders than the other frogs combined. Those who survived the battle ran for Prince Aldair's castle.

Just as Philip had said, Max had run off at the first sign of a fight. He had tried to find his way back to the place where he and Seth first met Samson, but he soon got completely and utterly lost. Famished, dehydrated, and overheated, he sat down. "What am I going to do?" he asked aloud.

A few hours later he started walking again. He found a nearby stream and got down on his knees. He was about to take a sip when he heard a voice from across the brook, "I wouldn't drink that if I were you."

"Why not?" inquired Max, locating the voice.

"Because, it is full of poisons," came the reply.

"But I am *so* thirsty."

"Come over here." Max crossed the stream and the man handed him a canteen, "Have some of my fresh water." Max gulped down all its contents.

His new acquaintance was short and scrawny, and Max thought he looked faintly familiar. Little did the teen know that this was one of Philip's men, an archer who had fled when his weapon had been shattered by a frog woman. It was not the first time the coward had fled from a fight. He had once been in the service of Smolden, but had abandoned the army when the dragon had actually sent them to fight. He was smart enough not to return to the underground, knowing that Smolden would have killed him for his cowardice.

As Max drank the water, the man was thinking how easy it was going to be to trap this young fool. The stream was, of course, not poisoned; he had gotten the water in his canteen from it. The boy, however, would soon learn to trust this caring and kind stranger. First the man would give him water, then he would complement the boy, and then ask him if he needed a guide. It was a perfect plan and he knew it would work. He hoped that bringing a new recruit would quench Smolden's anger.

"What is your name, lad?" he asked.

"Max," he replied.

"And what would bring a fine lad like you into these woods?"

"Well, I'm not sure. I woke up in the woods one day with my friend Seth and then he and I almost became princes. You see Samson the minotaur offered to let us come to his home with him..." Max began recounting the story of all that he had done since he woken on Issym. The stranger might have been a coward, but he was no fool. He could tell that this boy knew *the* Seth and Rachel and would be of extreme value to Smolden. *I'm going to get a huge reward!* he thought.

Chapter 9

It was decided that Princess Maria, Azmaveth, and Padon would stay in Prince Paseah's village. Flibbert, Seth, and Rachel bid them goodbye and were about to get on the road again when Philip appeared and asked, "May I come along?"

Flibbert answered harshly, "Definitely not." Rachel was glad Philip was not going to be allowed to join them, but Seth said, "I'm all right with it."

"Oh please let me; I promise you won't regret it," Philip begged.

"Why do you want to come?" Rachel questioned.

The thief shrugged. "I have nowhere to go and you guys seem like decent people."

She did not really want Philip to come, but if Seth trusted him, she would too. "As far as I'm concerned, you can come."

Flibbert finally gave in.

"How far is it to Universe Girl's house?" Rachel inquired as they started out.

"A few hours," Flibbert replied.

It was silent for most of their ride. The sky was dark as were their moods. Seth and Rachel were not used to sleeping in Xsardis; they were overtired and stiff from riding the horses and from yesterday's battle. Flibbert's heart was heavy for his brother and the village he had grown up in. Philip seemed deep in thought. Finally Rachel asked, "Seth, would you tell us more of the story?"

"Well..." he passed a hand through his hair, trying to surface. "We got up from lunch and kept walking. A fourth of the way up the mountain we paid another toll. That night we rested in a deep, narrow crag. I stood guard first and then Rachel did. It would have been foolish not to have posted a guard in such a place.

"In the morning we started our journey again." Seth stopped talking as the road curved and widened as white birch overtook the shady forest, allowing light to shine through. He saw a castle come into view. Tall and skinny, its size made it seem more like someone's home than a castle. Except for crystal towers, the regal structure was made of stone.

"Universe Girl's castle," Flibbert announced as he tethered his horse beside the front door. As they entered the dwelling, a girl who by the looks of her was about twenty-two was coming down the steps to meet them. She was wearing a floor-length dress. With long, brown hair and bright blue eyes that shone like the stars, something about her reminded Seth of an older Rachel. She descended the stairs with grace and stood before them. "Greetings," she said. "Good to see you again, Flibbert. You must be Rachel. And you are Seth, if I am correct?"

"How did you know?" Seth inquired.

"I know many things and I have a great number sources for the knowledge," the lady answered. "I am Universe Girl, but you may call me Ethelwyn—I prefer that name. Who is the other gentleman with you?"

"His name is Philip," Seth informed her.

"What can I do for you all?"

"We would like to go home."

"We need to bring two little girls who are staying with the airsprites and Seth's friend Max with us," Rachel added.

"Home?" she asked, color rushing to her face. "Already? You will not stay and help Issym?"

"We can't help Issym," Rachel replied. "We don't remember anything of value."

"Oh, but you know more than you think," Universe Girl told them.

"All the same," Rachel answered, "we would like to go home. It is my responsibility to make sure the twins get back to earth safely."

Ethelwyn hesitated for a minute and then she spoke, "Have lunch with me and then I will explain to you certain things."

Flibbert agreed, "Of course."

As Ethelwyn went into the kitchen to prepare lunch, Seth, Rachel, Philip, and Flibbert sat down in the living room and waited. No one said a word—they were all lost in their own thoughts. Rachel and Seth's minds rested on earth. *It won't be long before we're home again!* they both rejoiced. *Perhaps this is only a dream after all, and one that we will soon wake up from...*

After lunch had been served Seth asked, "So, will you send us home?"

Ethelwyn took a deep breath and finally answered, "I can't. It's not that I don't want to—I am not able." Rachel and Seth's eyes widened. "You see," she continued, "universes move and over time they drift from one of my orbs to the next. A long time ago one of my spheres was stolen. That orb now contains your universe."

It did not make sense. "But you brought us here, didn't you?" Seth questioned.

"Well, I brought Rachel. The airsprites came to me and told me that they wanted to summon her. I knew we had very little time before your universe drifted out of the orb I had, so without warning them that I wouldn't be able to take you back, I sent them to your world. Only minutes after the airsprites returned with Rachel, your universe disappeared from my ball and now lies only in the one orb that I don't have," she explained.

"Then who has it?" demanded Seth, indignant.

"Smolden."

"What!" exclaimed Flibbert hopping to his feet. "Wyn, what have you done?"

"How do we get home?" asked Rachel, hope draining from her. How could she explain to the twins that they were never going to see their parents again? How would her own parents handle their daughter being missing?

"You will have to recover the orb from Smolden the dragon."

"You can't be serious," Seth shook his head.

"That's impossible," Rachel had not been in Xsardis long, but she had already become well acquainted with the power and wickedness of Smolden.

Flibbert questioned, "Smolden can't be hurt by any known weapons. So how in Issym are they supposed to get him to surrender the sphere?"

"My suggestion is to visit the fairies," Universe Girl replied.

"They are on the other side of Issym!" the frog exclaimed.

"Yes, I know. I am terribly sorry to have brought this trouble upon you," Ethelwyn apologized. "The future of Issym depended on getting Rachel here. I knew that if I had been you, Rachel, I would have wanted someone to send for me if they thought I could help save a continent."

"I just wish I could have helped," Rachel answered.

Seth was not angry, but he was lost as to what to do, "We are only two teenagers. From what I understand, Smolden will stop at nothing to find us. How are we supposed to make it to the fairies?"

Flibbert declared, "I will speak with Ethelwyn alone. For now, rest. She and I will discuss your next steps."

Universe Girl led Flibbert upstairs to her study. As soon as the door was shut, the frog began to speak, "Ethelwyn, you are a woman of great wisdom. I do not begrudge you for the decision to bring Rachel, but are you sure there is no other way to get them home than to retrieve the orb from Smolden?"

"I know of none, old friend. I am truly sorry."

"Will the universe drift into one of the other orbs?" The frog paced the creaky, wooden floor that was covered in scrolls and books. Four desks and one long table filled the room that he knew well.

"If they had a hundred years to wait, possibly. But it could be even longer than that." Ethelwyn sat down, clearly troubled.

Flibbert stood beside a large window. He sighed, well aware that she was pained will guilt. "You are not to blame for this."

"Thank you, my friend, but I know that I am." She paused, "Perhaps it is destiny that they are not able to return to earth. Maybe God means for them to help us."

Flibbert crouched close to the ground, "Seth and Rachel are not what you would expect. I do not think they have the strength to war against Smolden."

"Sometimes I think frogs doubt other creature's hearts. If the teens were frogs, you would not speak of them the same way. You would defend their honor and courage."

"I don't know, Ethelwyn. They are very young and they do not seem to care about Issym."

"Do not judge them by what they are now. If they were strong enough to defeat Smolden, why would they need God? They may be weak, but that is when God is most strong! Do you not remember what God's Word says? 2nd Corinthians 12:9: 'But He said to me, "My grace is sufficient for you, for my power is made perfect in weakness. Therefore I will boast all the more gladly about my weaknesses, so that Christ's power may rest on me.'"

"Good verses, Wyn, but what is your point?"

"God's grace is sufficient for Issym and it is sufficient for Seth and Rachel. God's power is made perfect in weakness so maybe it is a good thing they are weak."

Flibbert had to admit that she was right. She was also correct when she pointed out that he would not think the same way if Seth and Rachel were frogs. A fly buzzed around Flibbert's head. His tongue shot out and the insect was no more. Universe Girl shook her head.

"You really want to send them to the fairies with no help?" he asked.

"Unless you wish to go with them…"

"I cannot. I have to warn the frogs of the upcoming battle."

"Not just frogs, Flibbert," Ethelwyn reminded him. "Humans too."

Flibbert shook his head. She was opinionated and stubborn, but perhaps that was why they were friends. The two had much more to discuss. There was no sense in disagreeing with her—he knew he would never prevail. When they finally descended to rejoin the others, the three humans were asleep on the couches.

Flibbert smiled and laid down on the other couch. *For once, he thought, there is no need of a night watch, which means...* Before he could finish his thought, Flibbert was asleep.

Sasha shifted into the form of a minotaur so she could blend in as she entered the underground. She walked for miles and finally arrived at a massive door. She addressed the two minotaur guards, "Let me pass. I have something to tell Lord Smolden."

Once inside, Sasha looked around her. She was familiar with Smolden's lair; she had been there several times. The room was massive. Behind Smolden she saw a deep lake. To his right and left, the dirt floor was lost beneath piles of treasure. But these jewels held no value to her. All Sasha was interested in for the moment was the ability to live forever, which is exactly what the leviathan Smolden had promised her, along with co-ruling Issym. She had little interest in sharing power.

Sasha morphed back into her preferred female, human self and stared up at the huge, black dragon. "I have heard some distressing news," growled Smolden, "news that you have lost my prisoner. Is this true?"

Sasha answered, "Yes. There were some complications."

"What kind of complications?"

"One of my own kind betrayed me and stole Seth and his friend. I'm sorry. It won't..."

"Never mind that now," Smolden cut in. "I received word that he didn't know anything of value anyway."

She had to wonder where he got his information. The dragon had more spies than she could guess. He seemed to be very persuasive. He was still confined to the underground and, yet, men and frogs and other creatures were joining up with him. What was it that made some fall easily to his charismatic nature and others rebel against it with all their hearts?

"I have a new task for you," he was saying.

Sasha's interest was instantly piqued. If Smolden had already moved on from her big mistake then there must be a very interesting plot forming in his mind.

The stranger had convinced Max to allow him to be his guide to Samson the minotaur's house. When they arrived, the two humans would go inside and down the steps leading to underground. Max would not be able to escape once he was there, and the man's reward would be for certain.

The stranger was thinking of his own wisdom when the house came into view. He started to walk in but Max stopped short, a sick feeling in his stomach. "Coming?" the man asked.

Max pushed aside all feelings that would have stopped him, nodded, and went in, taking a course of action that could never be undone.

Chapter 10

Those staying in the home of Universe Girl woke early the next morning. After breakfast, Ethelwyn supplied them with food and water for their journeys. Flibbert quickly bid them goodbye and rode away.

After he had gone, Ethelwyn took Seth and Rachel into her armory. "Take whatever you like," she offered. Seth chose a better sword; Rachel selected a dagger, a bow and some arrows, smiling as she thought, *It's just like in Seth's story.* Universe Girl handed them a map and gave them a few directions. Seth and Rachel saddled their horses and waved goodbye. Then they took one last look at Philip. Rachel was all too glad to say farewell. "Allow me to come with you, again," Philip addressed Seth.

Rachel rolled her eyes, "Why would we do that, Philip? We've already let you tag along this far." It was one thing to have him come when Flibbert was there to keep him in line but without the warrior frog, Rachel did not feel as secure.

"Because it isn't safe for two teenagers to go tramping about the woods by themselves. I can help you avoid dangers that would kill you if you were on your own. Plus, I grew up near the fairies so I can help keep you from getting lost."

He had a good list of reasons. His speech convinced even Rachel, though taking a criminal with them for protection would not be what either of them would have chosen under ordinary circumstances. He mounted a horse and they took off.

It was going to be a long ride, and Rachel figured that it was a good time for Seth to finish telling the story of when they climbed Mt. Smolden to find the gem of light. "So, did we succeed in climbing the mountain?"

"We sure did," Seth replied. "Snow started to fall and it got very cold. It was hard and rocky going but we climbed steadily up and up.

"A little past half way up the mountain a band of fourteen men surrounded us. 'You don't look like criminals,' they said.

"'We don't? But we are," I replied.

They answered, 'Prove it.'

"'Name your challenge,' I declared.

"'You any good with that bow, Missy?' he asked.

"Rachel, you added a snobby attitude as you told them, 'The best.'

"He ordered you, 'You see that bird? Shoot it. And you boy, you'll have to sword fight with Nekoda.' You pulled out your bow and strung an arrow as he continued, 'People have been trying to shoot the stupid bird for years. They say Smolden offers a reward to the person who succeeds. No one has been able to. It taunts us every day, swooping down and almost landing on our heads. It's almost like it's laughing at us.' He would have gone on to say more but you had already shot it. It fell with a screech.

"I pulled out my sword and so did the man who I guessed was Nekoda, but the leader stopped him. 'No, I'll fight the young man.' Apparently your shot had really impressed him. He never would have wasted his strength fighting me unless he thought that we were formidable enemies. I replied, 'Fine, but if that is to be the case let's put a wager on the fight.'

'What do you suggest?' he asked.

'If you win, you take my sword and the lady's bow, which is one of the finest ever crafted,' (the fairy Elaine had given it to you), 'and we retreat down the mountain, never to return again.'

'And we get to keep your packs,' he put in.

'Fine, but if *I* win you will give me your sword, follow us up the mountain making sure no one bothers us, *and* pay all the tolls it takes to get to our destination.'

'Deal,' he answered. He drew his weapon. 'Ready to give us the bow, Missy?" He was trying to act like he had the whole thing under control. I'll spare you the gory details, but I won the fight."

"So you really are *the* Seth and Rachel who created Xsardis?" Philip interrupted.

"I guess so," replied Seth, who with every passing second was growing in confidence that what he saw was real.

"Why did you want to come with us, Philip?" Rachel questioned again.

"Where else did I have to go? You guys seemed so kind and different from everyone else I know."

Rachel's heart softened to the bandit as the Holy Spirit, the voice of God and counselor to Christians, spoke to her heart. "Philip, we are no better than you on our own, but there is Someone who helps us to be better. He can help you too, if you want him too."

Philip's questioning face encouraged Seth to pick up where Rachel left off, "His name is Jesus Christ. He is the Son of the Almighty God. He came to earth and died upon a cross (a painful and humiliating way to die) for our sins, to make us clean and forgiven. No one deserves this gift but He gave it anyway. God raised Him from the dead after three days. Now we don't have to pay the penalty for our sins. If we just ask Jesus, He will come into our lives and wash away our sins so that we can have a relationship with God. Because Rachel and I have accepted the gift Jesus freely gave, we are different. He makes our lives better.

"God gave us a book so that we can get to know Him better and so that we know how to please Him and live rightly. It is called the Bible. In the Bible there are many smaller books, and one of them is called Romans. Romans 3:23 says, 'For all have sinned and fall short of the glory of God.' Romans 6:25 says, 'For the wages of sin is death but the gift of God is eternal life in Christ Jesus our Lord.' Acts is another smaller book in God's big Book. Acts 4:12 says, 'Salvation is found in no one else, for there is no other name under heaven given to men by which we must be saved,' (that's talking about Jesus.) And finally, Romans 10:9 says, 'That if you confess with your mouth Jesus is Lord and believe in your heart that God raised Him from the dead you will be saved.'

"We can be saved from our sins, which separate us from God, from the emptiness that each of us feel before Jesus comes into our hearts, from everything. Jesus is my best friend. He will be yours.

"Philip, do you believe that? If you do, all you have to do is talk to God like He is right here—which He is. Tell Him you are sorry for your sins and that you believe in Him. You can pray silently or out loud—it doesn't matter. God will hear you no matter what."

Philip turned his face from their view and both Rachel and Seth figured he was praying. Philip, however, was not praying. He was thinking, *These teens are crazy! All that stuff about Jesus and sins and God is way too weird for me. I'm going to go through with my original plan and deliver them over to Smolden.*

Kate and the rebel shape shifters had taken on the form of animals and traveled to Universe Girl's Castle. Once there, Kate morphed into the form of a human, while the rest stayed as they were. She knocked at the door. Ethelwyn opened it. "Can I help you?" she asked.

"I hope you will."

As soon as Max had descended the stairs leading to the underground, his guide's attitude had changed. The man had stopped treating Max like a friend and begun treating him like a prisoner. They walked for miles in the underground, until Max grew tired and begged for rest, but his "guide" refused to let him stop.

The first channel they had passed through had been short and narrow, but as they walked farther along the dirt floor, the rooms grew larger and taller. Tunnels appeared on either side of them. Max wondered where they led. Each room was dimly lit with torches on the walls.

It was humid and hard to breathe in the underground. The smell of smoke filled the air. Max could taste the sulfur. Occasionally holes above him let in some light and fresh air, but these were few and far between.

Max passed toads, humans, and minatours, all with snarls on their faces. The sounds of their bickering filled his ears. He heard metal clattering against metal. Occasional cries of pain rose above the din. What had he done by going to the underground?

Max thought to himself, *How could Seth abandon me? I bet he doesn't even know I'm missing. He's probably all caught up with Rachel! I can't believe I was ever friends with such a selfish boy. The first chance I have I'll get him back. See if I don't!*

They came to a huge door with two minotaur guards standing on either side. It was clear that minotaurs were the most honored of all the undergrounders, for everywhere Max had looked, minotaurs were giving orders to other creatures. "I'm taking him to see Smolden," his guide informed the guards, as he put his hand on his sword. The minotaurs snorted and didn't move. "He's of value. Now let me pass!"

"You don't order us, human!" growled a third minotaur, who was walking toward them. He looked Max over. "Value, eh? Give him to us; we'll see he gets to Lord Smolden."

The guide put his hand on Max's shoulder and squeezed so tightly it hurt the teen. "And let you take all the glory? I don't think so, Kreenar."

"Disobeying orders from a superior officer—that is punishable by death." Max began to think that there was going to be a fight. Apparently, all the nearby minotaurs thought the same thing, since they started pushing in around them.

"Oh you want to fight, eh? Fine," the human said, his voice growing loud. "I am sick of taking orders from you anyway." Every toad and human head in the room turned. "Its time someone stood up to you!" he shouted, and soon the toads and humans started pressing in on the minotaurs. Obviously no one liked taking orders from the beasts and would gladly rally around anyone who was going to stand up against them.

"Get back to your business," growled Kreenar.

The humans' and toads' answer was to draw their weapons.

"You all are guilty of insubordination!" shouted Kreenar. No one seemed to hear him. In frustration he ordered his minatours, "Attack!"

The fighting started, and Max found himself diving left and right, trying not to get killed. The battle did not last for more than a minute, because soon the massive door opened and a huge minotaur came out. At the sight of him the room went silent. "What is this all about?" boomed the new face. Kreenar and the man who had brought Max were quickly ushered forward. Both stood, looking very frightened, with no sound coming from their mouths. It was clear whoever this new minotaur was had power. "Well?" he demanded.

"I brought a boy to see Smolden." Max didn't like that he was being brought into this. He had hoped to slip out the back before anyone noticed him. "And *he* wouldn't let me through," whined the man, taking the classic route of blaming someone else.

Kreenar had to say something and fast, "Kerub…I… I offered to take the boy in myself, seeing as it was so important… but he accused me of trying to steal credit. Then he got all these humans and toads to attack us minotaurs."

"So this was all over who was going to get the glory?" The minotaur Kerub laughed, and everyone else laughed nervously with him. Then abruptly the laughter stopped and the minotaur leaned forward and said menacingly, "If this ever happens again the culprits will be killed on sight. Now you, Human, why is this boy so important?"

Max liked the sound of that question but not the sound of the answer, "He is friends with Seth and Rachel."

"I am not!" shouted Max. "I'm his ex-friend. I can't believe I ever spoke to that selfish…"

"Silence boy!" shouted Kerub. "You don't talk unless you are told to. Come forward now. I'll take you to Smolden." Both the human who had brought him and the other minotaur almost audibly complained. "If you have a problem with that, come and see Smolden yourself! We'll just see what he will do to anyone who questions the authority of his right hand."

Everyone in the room scattered at this and Max was pushed forward. With great anxiety he went through the door that he assumed would lead to Smolden.

Chapter 11

Max went through the massive door and what he saw knocked the wind right out of him. He stood in the presence Smolden the dragon. The beast's neck alone was over six feet tall and he was coal black from head to toe. Smolden's voice was deep and menacing, yet something in it called to Max. "Who is this?" the dragon questioned.

"His name is Max, sir. He came to Issym with Seth," answered Kerub the minotaur.

Smolden turned his attention to the boy standing beneath him. *Already,* mused the leviathan, *his fear of me is gone. His eyes and thoughts are on my gold and treasures. It won't be difficult to get him to cooperate.* He said aloud, "How would you like to go home, Boy?" Max looked up at the dragon, but gave no reply. "But not to go home as you are. No, I will send you to earth wealthy and powerful. Whatever you want will be given you."

Can this be true? Max asked himself. *Of course it is true. Why would Smolden lie to me? But what if the frogs were right? What if Smolden is an evil beast?*

"You have probably heard from those frogs that I want to take over Issym and that's true," Smolden continued. "But I only want back what is rightfully mine."

The smell in the room was sickly sweet. It made Max's head spin. He had trouble focusing on Smolden's words.

The dragon went on, "Issym was taken from me and now the world is in chaos. The people and frogs of this great continent need my help and I need your's. Will you help me to help them?"

Max pretended to think about the dragon had said but his mind was already made up. Wealth, power, and the chance to go home were knocking on his door. "Of course," he answered the dragon.

The smell in the lair had changed. It had turned into a pleasant and welcoming fragrance. Max's mind had turned clear and he longed to answer any questions Smolden might have.

"Tell me, Max, what was the last thing you remember while you were with Seth?"

"Well, he and I were traveling with a girl named Rachel and some frogs. A band, whose leader called himself Philip, attacked us. I ran off when the fighting started."

Smolden needed no more information for the moment. "I will call when I need more from you." He ordered Kerub the minotaur, "Make sure Max gets everything he wants. Then come back to me quickly."

So, brooded Smolden, *Rachel is here as well. This might make things more complicated.*

The minotaur led Max out of the room. *Seth and that stupid frog Flibbert were wrong,* the teen thought to himself. *Smolden is going to treat me well.*

Kerub returned to his master swiftly. He bowed and asked Smolden, "Your orders, sir?"

"Search for a message from Philip," the dragon commanded.

Kerub hurried out of the room. He needed to check the message drops, holes in Issym that allowed the dragon's spies to feed him information. There were many of the openings in the underground, so he enlisted several other minotaurs to help him. Finally Kerub found the letter from Philip. He returned to Smolden's lair, glad to bring good news. "Philip has told us where he is taking Seth and Rachel."

"Good," Smolden declared. "Take some troops and go intercept them."

"So what happened next in the story?" asked Rachel as she, Seth, and Philip traveled along the road, on their way to the mushnicks and fairies. The narrow path was overgrown with plant life. Philip was in the lead; Seth rode in the middle; and Rachel was in the rear.

They seemed to go very slowly and Rachel wondered why. Surely the horses could move faster. She wished Philip would urge his animal onward. She wanted to get home as quickly as possible. Rachel sighed. At least it was a nice day.

There was not a cloud in the sky and the sun shone so brightly Rachel had to squint to see. She drew a deep breath. Her lungs felt tired. She decided just to close her eyes for a moment, let her horse follow Seth and Philip, and listen to the tale Seth was telling.

"We traveled on with the men," he began. "They kept their end of the bargain. They paid our tolls and insured that no one bothered us. The farther we traveled up Mt. Smolden the fewer people we saw, but each group we did meet was more fierce than the one before it.

"There were four toll points on the mountain. We had already passed three. Only a very select few got passed the last point, because it led to Smolden's lair.

"We neared the summit. Eight men stood up from the ground when we approached. They declared, 'No one goes past here. This is the domain of Smolden the dragon. Turn around.'

"I pulled out my sword and so did the fourteen men who traveled with us. The eight who stood in our way readied their own weapons.

"The leader of the band we were traveling with replied, 'Let them pass. The girl shot the eagle and you know as well as I do that Smolden said the person who killed it would be welcomed in his home. Even he couldn't kill that stupid bird. 'Sides if you don't let them through, they'll be a fight and I can guarantee you, you don't want that.'"

"'Alright then. Because she shot the bird, we will let you in for the small sum of three-hundred gold pieces,' they responded.

"The men we were traveling with handed over the large price. Rachel and I moved up the mountain. We would go on alone for the rest of our journey."

Seth, Philip and Rachel broke for a quick lunch as Seth stopped speaking. Unpacking some food from their bags, they heard footsteps rushing towards them. Seth and Rachel jumped to their feet and drew their weapons, but Philip stayed seated. "Don't run," he declared. "It'll only make things worse."

"You cowardly traitor!" shouted Rachel, as she grasped the situation.

"Don't call me such names, Missy. You knew when you brought me along that I was a criminal," Philip replied.

"We've got to try to get away from here," Seth told Rachel. He was as furious as she was, but he knew that they did not have time to waste on fighting with Philip. Rachel and Seth started to run.

Within a few minutes, Seth was tired but Rachel was much worse. She was gulping the air, and beginning to slow her pace. Soon Rachel collapsed to the ground, her breaths short and heavy. Seth stopped running and knelt over her. She was barely conscious. What had happened?

Seth heard his pursuers' footsteps getting closer and knew that they had to run. "Can you move at all?" he asked Rachel. She shook her head.

His eyes darted around the forest, desperate for some kind of hiding place. The tree beside him had low branches and lots of leaf coverage. *Perhaps, by God's grace, the undergrounders won't look up,* Seth hoped. He scurried up the first branch and asked Rachel for her hand. She used the last of her strength to give it to him and he pulled her up. Seth lifted her to next branch and the next and only stopped when he saw seven minotaurs and Philip racing by. They did not even glance upwards. When they were gone, Seth let go of the breath that he had not known he had been holding. *Thank you God!*

It was over an hour before Rachel managed speak. "Seth," was her first word.

"Are you alright?" he asked from his position on a nearby branch. Seth had judged half an hour ago when her breath had become easier and her color had begun to return that she was out of danger.

"My asthma has never gotten this bad, this quickly before."

They did not speak again. Seth thought it would be safer to spend the night in the tree. What if the undergrounders doubled back? Sleeping on a branch would not be very comfortable, but safety needed to be their first priority.

How will we ever make it to the fairies? Seth asked himself. *Rachel can't run for ten minutes without almost dying, our guide is a traitor, and we are just two lost teenagers. Max has run off, Flibbert's gone, and we can't go home because of an evil dragon.*

What are we going to do?

Sasha left the underground and shifted into the form of a cloud. In this form she observed everything that the airsprites did. That night, when they were all asleep, she turned back into her human form and walked into the castle of the airsprites. Her objective, given to her by Smolden, was to discover the gem of light's location.

Sasha was not even noticed as she entered the castle and thought to herself, *No soldiers guard the home of the queen! How naïve. This will be easier than I thought!*

Entering the queen's bedroom and putting a knife to her throat, Sasha whispered in her evil but beautiful tones, "Tell me where the gem of light is."

Interestingly, Sasha's mistake had almost worked to Smolden's advantage. Smolden had made it known some time ago that he was going to head for Kembar plains. Normally, he kept his plans secret as long as he could, knowing that with many men come many spies; but in this case, he wanted Issym to know that he was going to attack. He wanted the people scared. He wanted them, by trying to protect themselves, to actually hurt themselves. His greatest wish was that every creature in Issym would rush to the fairies to protect them. And while all their attention was there, Smolden would take the gem of light and make sure no one ever found it.

Although the dragon had made it known that he was going to attack the fairies, at first the people of Issym had done nothing more than increase the guard at the underground entrance. He had succeeded in frightening the people, but they were not rallying to protect the fairies. Until Seth and Rachel came along.

The teens made the people of Issym feel invincible. Now, confident that they could defeat Smolden, they headed for the land of the fairies. Good. Now all the dragon needed was for Sasha to discover the gem, cover it so that it would not hurt him and bring it to the underground. Smolden would bury it deep beneath the ground where it could not affect him and where no one would ever find it.

The thought of sending Sasha to retrieve the gem was horrifying. Giving his most formidable enemy/ally the power to destroy him was not a good plan, but what choice did he have? As long as the gem of light shone brightly, Smolden could never go out of the underground. Horrid gem! Once Smolden had loved the waters above the ground. It had been his only joy. But the jewel had stolen that pleasure from him, turning its waters poisonous to the dragon. Soon Issym would rue the day it had made an enemy of Smolden the leviathan.

Chapter 12

"What a beautiful day God has made! What a lovely morning He's given us!" sang a voice. Seth could hear a flute pick up the tune as the man's voice ceased and he came into view. Rachel stirred and was about to speak but Seth put his finger to his lips. He was glad to see that Rachel had color in her face and wanted to ask her how she was doing, but they couldn't risk making any sound until this man had gone by. What if he worked for Smolden?

The flute played a cheerful little tune, and Seth saw that the man behind it was tall, lean, and strong, with a slightly shaggy goatee. A horse ambled along beside him, loaded with a sword, a bow, a quiver full of arrows, and various other bundles. The man, despite his weapons, did not seem menacing.

He stopped playing and walking when he saw Seth and Rachel sitting in a tree. "Good morning," he greeted them cheerfully.

Seth was hesitant to trust anyone at this point, but saw little option but to reply, "Good morning."

Rachel was bolder, not believing that anyone who looked as happy as this man could be an enemy. "I am Rachel and this is Seth. Who are you?"

"My name is Galen. Say, you wouldn't be the Seth and Rachel who came up with the ideas for this place would you?"

Seth wouldn't have answered that question but he couldn't silence Rachel. She saw Galen's kind eyes and trusted him immediately —she had always believed you could tell a lot about a person by his eyes. "Yes, actually, we are," she answered. "But why do you say the *ideas* for this place?"

"Certainly you don't believe that you are responsible for the creation of Issym and Asandra. You came up with the ideas for Xsardis, that's true, but God created the world. He made the trees, the sun and the moon; He created the frogs, the mushnicks and all the creatures; He gave the fairies and the shape shifters their abilities. In short, you two imagined Xsardis—God created it."

With a cocked head Galen asked, "Why are you sitting in a tree?"

"We were chased by a pack of minotaurs," Seth informed him. "We ran for a little while but had to stop when Rachel couldn't breathe."

"I see. But why are you out in the woods all by yourselves?"

"Our guide turned out to be our enemy. Now we are alone, heading to a place we've never been before—to the land of the fairies and mushnicks," Rachel replied.

"Would you care to join me for breakfast?" Galen invited.

"Yes please," Seth accepted.

"So, may I ask where you are going, Galen?" Seth inquired, biting into an apple, after he and Rachel had climbed out of the tree.

"Nowhere in particular," came the reply. "I mostly just wander around. I meet some pretty interesting people this way."

"Don't you have a home?" asked Rachel.

"Oh yes, back at Fort Misson. My father rules the fort. I left a couple of years ago."

"Why? Did you have a fight with your father?" Seth questioned.

"Goodness no. My father and I had a good relationship, but I had lived all my life at the fort, only stepping outside it to hunt or fish. It was time for me to see the world so that I could be a better ruler when the time came for me to take control of the fortress.

"I felt God's tug on my heart to go wandering. So I took some food, a sword, a bow, some arrows, a little bit of money, and my flute and hit the road.

"Someday, when I am ready, and God tells me to, I'll go back. Until then, I wander. I've been able to do a lot of good, helping lost people and defending travelers from bandits. I feel like I have a purpose even though it looks like all I do is amble around.

"But don't you miss your friends?" Rachel inquired.

"Absolutely, but I have to press on. I think I'll know when it is time to go back home," Galen answered.

"You must get so lonely!" exclaimed Seth.

"Oh, I do but God gives me good company," replied the future fort ruler.

Galen was gaining more of Seth's trust, so the teen told him about how he and Rachel had come into Issym. He also informed Galen that they didn't feel they could help Issym and why they were going to the fairies.

"Now," said Galen as he picked up from breakfast, "since you lost your guide, you probably would like some help finding the fairies. I would be honored if you would let me accompany you."

"Only if it wouldn't be to much trouble," replied Seth, trying to be polite but ever so glad Galen had offered. Even with Universe Girl's map, he had was not sure how he would find the fairies, and there was also some comfort in having a skilled fighter in the group.

"Good. Lets get started."

Flibbert rode from frog village to frog village, trying to raise an army to fight Smolden the dragon. Few refused to help; they all knew the gravity of the news Flibbert brought.

The fourth village he stopped at was ruled by an old frog named Marvin. He and his granddaughter Amber had been friends of Flibbert's family since Flibbert and Amber were children. When Flibbert arrived, Amber came out to meet him. "Greetings, Flibbert the frog," she welcomed. "Do you come with good news?"

"I'm afraid not, Lady Amber. Smolden is planning an attack and is rallying at Kembar plains. I am traveling around raising an army to fight the dragon. We need all the help we can get. I am sending everyone who will aid our cause to meet at Prince Aldair's castle."

"Have you asked the human villages yet?"

"No. I'm working my way up from Finrod's village and haven't come to any yet. But time is short. Do you really think it's worthwhile to go to them?

"Absolutely. But you're right. You probably won't have time to reach every village, so I'll ride ahead of you passed the Great Line," she answered, speaking of the imaginary line that divided Issym in half. "I'll rally support from the human and frog villages there."

Inside Flibbert smiled. Outside he declared, "No way."

"Why not? Because I'm a girl? Come on Flibbert! It's just like you to be so pigheaded," she rolled her eyes. "I'm a fast rider."

Flibbert would have fought with her, but he knew that the delay was not worth it. Amber would not be dissuaded. They had been friends for too long for him to believe he could stop her from doing anything she set her mind to.

"Fine, but be careful. You do realize the risk, don't you? Who knows what Smolden is planning? Who knows the dangers?"

"I understand. Should I send those I rally to Aldair?"

"Since you'll be speaking with those past the Great Line I think that you should send them straight to the fairies."

"It makes good sense." With that, Amber gracefully sprang off to ready her horse and to speak with her grandfather.

Flibbert left the village and traveled on, getting more and more support. However, when he reached the village of Prince Edgar, he knew that he was going to have difficulty convincing the frogs there to help.

Saying a prayer he entered the village.

Max walked through the underground with a swagger. All his life he had been a shadow, of Seth or someone else. The second best on the basketball team; the back up guitar player; the cool guy's best friend; the pretty girl's boyfriend (that never lasted). But in the underground, he felt like someone. He was helping a mighty dragon conquer a continent. *Beat that Seth!* he said.

He looked at the highly ornamented clothing he was wearing and compared himself to the minatours, toads and humans in rusting armor and muddy pants and ragged shirts. He was no one's shadow.

Rounding a corner, he came face to face with the man who had brought him to the underground. Anger flared within him. This human had pushed and pulled him all through the underground, treating him like a slave. "Why is this man not in chains?" he demanded of a nearby minatour.

The minatour grunted, "I don't know," and quickly moved away.

"In case you didn't know," Max sharply declared to the man before him, "I am very important to Smolden. I'm going to go to him this instant and tell him to punish you."

The human shrugged. "Your funeral."

Max tried to sound threatening. "Excuse me?"

The human laughed. "He's puffed your head up pretty big. But go ahead; go before the dragon uncalled for. See what he does."

Max stormed off. As he approached Smolden's lair he saw a large minatour coming out. It was Kerub, the dragon's second in command. Seeing Max, Kerub ordered, "Come here. Smolden wishes to hear the rest of your tale."

The teen willingly complied. He bowed before the dragon, "Thank you for your gifts, Lord Smolden."

The leviathan waved a paw through the air, "It is nothing. Now, tell me what more you know."

Max related everything he could think of.

"That is all. You may go."

The teen turned to leave and then thought better of it. "My lord?"

"What is it?" Impatience was clear in the dragon's voice.

"The man who brought me here..."

"What of him?"

"He was very cruel to me. I can't see why he should be allowed to go free."

"Consider the matter taken care of. Kerub, see to it."

"Thank you my lord." Max smiled. If this is what power felt like, it worth anything to get.

With deep anguish someone was hollering his name. It was so loud. He could not escape it. The undergrounders would probably praise him for what he had done, but somehow that did not ease his discomfort. What would happen to the man who screamed his name? What would happen to the man he handed over to the wrath of Smolden for the sake of revenge?

Max bolted upright. Sweat was pouring from him. His stupid conscience! He fell back onto his bed.

No. He could not sleep. He sat up, and slipped his feet into his expensive slippers. Then he pulled on his bear skin robe and reached under his pillow for a sack of golden coins Smolden had given him.

This was the power he had longed for? It certainly did not feel very good. He knew that to become anyone great on Issym or earth he would have to get rid of his conscience. How hard could that be?

He made up his mind. The man had deserved the trouble. He had brought it upon himself. Max had done what was just. He would not allow himself to feel guilty about it.

Chapter 13

Galen and Seth were walking, while Rachel rode the only horse the company had (though this was against her will). As they traveled, the new friends began to trade stories. "Seth has been telling me the tale of when we climbed Mt. Smolden," Rachel told Galen.

"Ah yes," the man replied. "I am familiar with that tale."

"Would you like to know the end?" Seth asked Rachel. She nodded and so he told her, "After we had passed the last group of guards we did not see anyone for miles. I'm sorry to say that this story has kind of a boring ending."

"What do you mean?" she inquired.

"Well, apparently no one is foolish enough to steal from Smolden and even if they were, they would never get by the fourth set of guards, so the dragon never even hesitated to leave his treasures unprotected when he flew away for one reason or another."

"And?"

"He, just, wasn't there when we went into his cave. So we walked through his domain and found the gem of light. It was covered by a thick blanket so that its light wouldn't affect Smolden. We carried the gem out. The fairies had given us a stone that would grant us the power to transport back to them, so we used it, gave them the gem, and they sent us home."

"That's it?" Rachel asked, realizing how much her story making skills had improved since she was a kid.

"Yep."

"So, Galen," Rachel started, switching topics, "tell us about your life at Fort Misson, or about your travels since you left."

"Let's see," Galen replied. "I must think of something interesting to tell you. Oh, you'll like this story. One day, I was eating lunch at a village near Mt. Smolden. The village had a guard stationed on its outskirts and I was eating with him, helping him keep guard."

"Could one or two guards really do a lot against the villains that go up Mt. Smolden?" Rachel inquired.

"No, but if some men from the mount decide to attack the village, the guard can alert the town. Or if someone has been kidnapped and men are dragging him or her up the mountain, the guard will alert the village and the town can try to mount a rescue.

"While I was eating with this middle-aged guard, we heard a great ruckus near the mountain (for the town is very close to the mountain and the guard's house is only a few hundred yards away). We looked out the window and saw that a woman was being dragged up the mountain. She put up quite the fight, but she was no match for the seven men that pushed and pulled her up.

"The guard was ready to call the town and form a rescue party, but I launched myself out of the house towards the mountain. I wanted to get to her as quickly I could. The guard, seeing my rash action, followed. We dealt with the kidnappers and brought the girl back to the village."

"Who was she?" Rachel asked.

"Her name was Andrea and she was the most beautiful woman on Xsardis, in my opinion." Galen answered, with a face full of a happy memory. "Well, I've told you a story. It's time for you to tell me one of yours."

Rachel and Seth wanted to ask why she had been captured, but they did not think it polite so they told one of their own stories, and in this way, they walked on quite happily for two days.

Galen had been kind enough to share his provisions, but they were running low. They knew as they sat down for lunch on the third day of their travels with Galen that the meal would be scarce.

They divided up the last of the food. Seth, Rachel and Galen did not say anything. Galen felt badly that he was out of food for them;

Seth and Rachel worried because they had taken all his provisions. In the silence, the chirping of the birds could be heard and the... "Did you hear that?" Rachel asked the question quickly.

"Minatours; a large group of them by the sound of it," Galen determined. "We have to go."

They did not gather up the little food they had; they simply ran. Galen told them to leave the horse behind—where they were going, she would only slow them down.

They had to get off the path. The three humans ran into the woods. They could not afford the time to look behind them; they had to watch their step and move any branches that blocked their path. Seth thought they could move no slower. His heart was racing.

Galen led Seth and Rachel expertly and they came out in just a few minutes time on a new path—it was small and overgrown, but they would make better time on it than they had in the thick of the woods. Seth had no idea if they were actually being followed or if they had lost their pursuers.

They started to run. Seth liked the feel of exerting himself. It was apparent that Rachel did not. The color in her face disappeared. Her eyes rolled back into her head. In another moment she collapsed to the ground.

Not again, he thought, dropping to her side.

Galen quickly looked her over. Her breathing was shallow and her face was pale. "We've got to get her help. Follow me," Galen ordered, picking up Rachel and starting to run.

Seth did not question the man. He sprinted alongside Galen until a cave came into view. By now even their breathing was heavy, and Seth was all too happy when Galen declared, "We go in."

But what Galen asked next scared Seth, "Do you trust me?"

Why would he ask me this now? What lies in that cave? Seth wondered.

The teen thought about it for a moment. This was no small question. The people you absolutely trust are to be treasured and few— and *real.* Up until now Seth could still say that he believed everything in this world to be nothing more than a dream, but if he said he trusted Galen, Seth was admitting that Xsardis actually existed. Was he really willing to accept that he was in a world he created as a kid? Was he really willing to trust Rachel's life to this man? The thoughts flashed through his mind in a moment; then he answered, "Yes."

"Then no matter what we encounter, don't run."

Flibbert entered the village that he knew would offer no help to his cause. The huts formed a circle with an empty middle. Frogs bustled about, doing their daily duties, and at first no one paid any attention to him. After a few minutes a frog woman looked at him suspiciously, and not recognizing him, stopped what she was doing and stared at him until others began to pay attention too. Soon the whole village had stopped and was staring at him. Flibbert rode his horse into the middle of the circle.

A family that for generations had showed no concern for what was right, but only for what was easy and profitable, ruled the village. Most of the frogs did not fight against their ruler's will and those who did were imprisoned. Flibbert doubted he would have an easy time getting this group of frogs to fight against Smolden, since the royal family supported undergrounder take over. Nevertheless, Flibbert began to speak, "Fellow frogs, it is time to make a stand." All eyes were on him and every ear listened. "Smolden is planning to make an attack on Issym. Unless we rally together, we will be defeated and he will subdue Issym, making all of us his slaves and servants. Not only that, but if he takes this land, Asandra will soon fall. It is obvious that his rule will not benefit us; long, long ago, before the gem of light came into the airsprites' hands, he ruled this world and we were all oppressed." Flibbert's voice rose in intensity as he spoke, "Then the mushnicks, frogs, humans, airsprites, and fairies joined together and fought against the powers of darkness and overcame them with the help of the Almighty God. We must not let their hard work be in vain—we must fight against Smolden again, and this time, defeat him once and for all!"

Word that Flibbert was speaking reached the ears of the village leader, Prince Edgar, and he came out to listen. He was dressed in a long purple robe. In most frog villages, if a leader wore anything but battle armor it was disgraceful. The robe was a sign of peace and comfort and armor was a sign of readiness. A ruler was considered great if he truly was always ready to protect his frogs and so most frog leaders wore only armor in public. But Prince Edgar had done away with this tradition and wore a robe. When Flibbert saw this he inwardly gagged and almost stopped speaking. *The cowardice of this leader!* he thought to himself.

He managed to continue speaking. "Frogs and humans are rallying together to fight against this evil! Will you join them?" he asked, looking into their eyes, hoping to appeal to what their hearts knew was right over what their minds and fellows and rulers told them.

At first it looked as if the frogs might join him, and Flibbert felt a spark of hope. But the village ruler laughed mockingly. "Who do you think you are, frog," he chuckled, "that you come here and disturb my frogs with such nonsense?"

"I am Flibbert and I beg you, please listen to me. We need your help. Will you leave your fellow frogs to fight this battle while you stay and hide?" Flibbert questioned, trying to appeal to the village's honor. Unfortunately, the frog he spoke to did not care about his own honor let alone the honor of his village. Prince Edgar thought he and his town were more sophisticated than the rest of the frog villages and cared nothing for them.

"What makes you think Smolden will wage a war with you, and even if he does why do you assume he will rule us cruelly?" Prince Edgar inquired.

Flibbert was about to answer but the ruler continued. *Apparently that was a rhetorical question,* Flibbert mused.

"No, we won't waste our time helping you. We are too busy. What, do you think we can all leave our jobs behind and go on fool's errands? Go away, frog, bother another village." The prince turned and went into his house. Frogs started to go quietly back to their work. A few glanced at him with remorse in their eyes. They knew they should help, but without approval from others, they would not.

Flibbert should have left, but he knew that every warrior counted. He jumped off his horse, landed, and shouted to the villagers, "Wait! You must listen to me. We need your help! Please, come to the aid of your fellow frogs!" His calls were useless; the bustle of the village had started again, leaving Flibbert with a heavy heart.

Universe Girl stood at her door and stared past the woman standing there to the animals behind her. At first Ethelwyn was confused, and then she realized that they were shape shifters. Her eyes widened and she thought about running but knew that there was no point.

Kate noticed Ethelwyn's fear and told her, "We don't want to hurt you."

"Then what do you want?" she questioned.

"May we speak with you?"

The shape shifters took on the form of humans and frogs and went inside the castle. Kate introduced herself and those with her to Universe Girl. Then she told Ethelwyn, "We are not like other shape shifters; we do not want to hurt anyone. That's why we left our people. We desire to help you in the battle against Smolden."

The airsprites' queen, Danielle, refused to tell Sasha the shape shifter where the gem of light was. Sasha fumed inwardly. She had hoped that she would simply be able to find out where the gem was and bring it down to Smolden. Now she would have to do things the hard way.

Tying up the queen tightly, Sasha hid her in one of her secret lairs in the ground of Issym. Then she took on Queen Danielle's form. *I'll have to play the part of the queen and discover where the gem is on my own,* planned Sasha.

Max had been enjoying life as a prince in the underground. He was dressed well, fed well, and treated well by the troops. At first he thought, *I'll never go home again. There is no school here, no parents to tell me what to do, and no bossy friends like Seth.* But he soon got bored. Though Smolden's troops feigned respect for him, they were not good for company, and with nothing else to do he just sat around all day. Finally he decided to explore the underground.

While going into a side passage that was rarely used, he came upon a room that was supposed to be locked. The lock, however, was not tight and Max opened it and went inside the room.

As he opened the door he saw walls made of bricks and bars that created yet another room, in which a prisoner sat. There were a few barrels outside this jail cell, but nothing else could be found in the room.

It was obvious that at one time the prisoner's clothes had been costly. The deeply colored cloth was torn and mud-stained. The man had been there, judging from his beard, for several months at least. New and old wounds could be seen all over him as he looked up at Max. At first his eyes showed defiance and rage. But, taking note of his visitor's weak, pampered manner and embellished clothing, the prisoner realized that Max was not one of Smolden's hardened officers. His eyes lightened to compassion. Max was puzzled. Why should the man have sympathy for him? He was not the one in a jail cell.

The man shook his head and said, "He's trapped another."

"What do you mean?" inquired Max.

"You—he's trapped you."

"Who's trapped me?" Max snorted.

"Smolden." Max's eyes were full of questions, so the man continued. "Smolden has tricked you into helping him, hasn't he?"

"I am helping him but he hasn't tricked me into anything. Issym was taken from him and he wants it back because the people are destroying it and need guidance." *Why am I explaining myself to him?* Max asked himself.

The prisoner took a breath and then started talking so fast Max could barely keep up with his words, "Listen up lad, for I have much to tell you and little time to do it. Smolden is not what he appears. It is true that he once ruled the world *but* in those days he enslaved the people and all things teetered near destruction. We freed ourselves and confined him here. Now he is trying to take Issym again. I don't know who you are or why you are helping him, but you must stop."

"Hey…"

"Go, now, before they see me talking to you." Max stumbled out of the room. *That was strange,* he thought.

Chapter 14

Seth got a sickly feeling in his stomach as he heard Galen say the words, "Then no matter what we encounter, don't run." What could that mean? Was he putting Rachel's life in danger? *Well,* thought Seth, *I told him I trusted him and now I must.* So he pushed back his fears and followed Galen into the cave.

It was extremely large, and a fire inside provided light. As they entered the cavern, Seth did come very close to running. Standing in front of him was a troll! He was as large as a house, was gray in color, and had a head the size of a boulder. The troll had its back to them and apparently did not know anyone was there.

Galen, showing no fear, stepped forward and greeted, "Orvan!"

The troll turned and looked surprised, "Visitors." After taking a closer look he questioned, "Galen, is that you my old friend?" His friendly tone contrasted his frightening appearance.

"It is, Orvan. How have you been?"

"All right—a little lonely, but all right. Who have you brought with you?"

"This is Seth and the lady in my arms is Rachel."

"And what seems to be the matter with the lady?" asked Orvan.

Galen did not want to answer this in front of Seth. "We need food," he started, "and water."

"My home is always open," Orvan replied, figuring Galen would answer him when the time was right.

Galen set Rachel down by the fire and checked her pulse. He knew that she would not make it through the evening—the disease spread too rapidly.

He put water to Rachel's lips and poured it down her throat. Seth sat beside her. Galen moved to stand near Orvan. The mighty troll gently picked Galen up and put him on his shoulder so they could talk without Seth hearing. What Galen whispered, Seth could not distinguish, but his tones were grave. The teen turned his eyes toward Rachel. Her whole body was trembling. Seth removed the cloak Universe Girl had given him and laid it over her.

Orvan set Galen down and disappeared deeper into his cave. When he came back, he was carrying something. "Boy," he said, indicating Seth. "I wonder if you might put this on the lady's neck. If she wakes up, she might enjoy looking at it."

Orvan put his hand low enough for Seth to reach into it; he was holding a necklace. The teen glanced up at the him. The troll's face was sad.

He examined the necklace. It had a silver chain and a small vial full of sparkling blue dust hanging from it. He clasped it on Rachel's neck.

Swallowing hard, Seth asked Galen, "What's wrong with her?"

Galen took a breath before he answered. "She has a disease called acena. It attacks people in the places of their body where they might be a little weaker than normal. For example, someone with bad eyesight who caught the disease might go completely blind."

"Rachel has asthma; the disease attacked her lungs," Seth said, beginning to piece things together. All the times Rachel had seemed exhausted after a short walk, more and more color draining from her face every day, the times she had collapsed from lack of oxygen— everything seemed so clear now. "What will happen to her?" he asked.

"The disease is so strange; it never affects two people the same way. So we can't be sure," Galen replied. "The more Rachel does, the worse her condition will get. Eventually, she won't be able to take a breath.

"If we had understood what was happening sooner, we could have forced her to rest and kept her alive, but now I fear that acena has too great a hold on her for us to do anything. In a few hours time, she may die."

Seth, Galen, and Orvan sat in the troll's cave for the rest of the afternoon. No one talked much—they were all too busy praying and thinking. Seth and Galen did, however, manage to fill Orvan in on who Seth and Rachel were, how they had come to Issym and where they were going.

Evening came and the fire was the only light in the cave. Seth poked at his food but could not eat; his heart was too heavy. He glanced at Rachel and thought he heard a moan.

He thought she was trying to sit up. "Rachel!" he exclaimed as adrenaline rushed through his body.

Seth scampered over to her and helped her sit up. She rested in his arms. "What happened?" she muttered. "Where are we?"

All eyes were fixed on Rachel. She looked pale, but much better than she had an hour ago. She was no longer trembling and her breath was deeper. "What?" Galen breathed, unable to believe his eyes.

Rachel scanned the room and her glance fell on Orvan. Fear came over her and she clutched Seth's arm. *A troll! All trolls are evil. We must be prisoners. How are we going to get out of here?*

"He's our friend," Seth told her quickly.

Rachel looked at the troll skeptically and asked Seth, "Are you sure?"

"Positive." Rachel did not let go of his arm.

Galen now spoke, "He's an old friend of mine and gave us shelter. Somehow you caught acena—a deadly a virus; that was why it was so hard for you to breathe. You fell unconscious. We brought you here as quickly as we could."

"Why *here?*" she questioned, looking at Seth.

"We had to get away from the minatours. Orvan has been very good to us." He tried to comfort her fears.

In the silence that followed, Galen inquired of Orvan, "Have you ever known anyone to recover from acena like this?"

The troll's eyes were looking at them, but his focus was elsewhere. "I didn't know if the necklace would work and I didn't want to get your hopes up. Long ago, I met a lady fairy. She was beautiful and was a fairy of the blue." (God created fairies with two different abilities. Blue fairies can heal and green fairies have extra strength.)

"I don't know why she loved me, but she did. One day on her way to visit me, she was attacked. I came to her defense and killed most of the villains but I was too late. I picked her up in my hands and she told me she loved me. Then she took a vial from her neck and cried her magical tears into it. She sealed the bottle so that it would never open and then breathed her last." A moment of silence followed. "That is the necklace you wear. I could only hope it would heal you."

Rachel took her hand off Seth's arm—she wasn't afraid anymore.

Universe Girl and the shape shifters who had broken off from Edmund talked for several hours. After they had spent some time together, Ethelwyn decided to give them her trust. They were indeed shape shifters, but she made it a habit not to judge by outside appearances.

Universe Girl liked Kate. She seemed courageous and intelligent. Courageous because she had left Edmund's control and intelligent because she had brought her shape shifters here. Ethelwyn's was a logical stop. If she trusted them, then all Issym would follow suit. Kate also led *and* listened well. She claimed not to be the leader of the shape shifters—that they had no leader—but she was the spokesperson and everyone followed her advice. It had been her idea, too, to break off from Edmund.

Universe Girl informed them, "Everyone is rallying at Prince Aldair's castle."

"Why? Smolden's troops are going to Kembar Plains." Kate did not question Ethelwyn's words; she simply did not understand.

"The castle is near the middle of Issym. It is a good halfway point. You should go there."

"But will they trust us?"

"No; not unless I give you a letter to present to Aldair."

"Will you?"

She was already reaching for paper, "Of course."

In the little over a week that Max had been in the underground, Smolden had only sent for him a few times, but when the dragon had, Max wished that he had not. Smolden asked questions about Issym and Seth and Rachel that Max did not know the answers to. And when Max had not give answers to Smolden's satisfaction the dragon turned from kind host to raging captor.

In only a few days, Max had gone from being treated like royalty to being treated like dirt. Instead of eating as much as he liked and having anything he wanted, he would lay awake hungry and cold at night. Max wanted to leave the underground, but knew that Smolden would never allow him to. He now understood why the prisoner he had met the other day had pitied him.

Max had decided to visit the prisoner, whose name was Arvin, every day. It was the only pleasurable thing to do in the underground. "Why are you locked in here, anyway?" Max asked.

"My father was one of the leaders of the resistance against the dragon before Seth and Rachel took the gem of light and gave it to the airsprites, forcing Smolden to make the underground his home," Arvin replied. "I continued in my father's steps, taking every opportunity I got to fight Smolden. I dissuaded men from joining his ranks, and fought his army whenever bands of them came aboveground.

"Long has there been a price on my head. Smolden offered great riches and his favor to anyone who would bring me to the underground. One day I went to visit a frog village. The prince bound me and sent me here."

"Guess I was right about those frogs... you can't trust them."

"There are humans that you can trust and humans that you can't. And there are frogs that you can trust and frogs that you can't. I know a lot of good frogs..."

"Well I don't. And that Flibbert, he is a trouble maker, I can tell."

Arvin sighed, "Flibbert's one of the best frogs I know, but he can seem..."

"Prideful, irritating, selfish, domineering.."

"Okay, okay, I get it. Your first impression wasn't the best."

"Yeah; you could say that."

Arvin was aware that trying to convince Max of anything would do more harm than good. "Why don't you go back before someone comes looking for you."

It was strange for Max to take orders from a person *inside* a prison cell, but somehow he could not help it. Arvin had a persuasiveness about him and a kindness that made the teen want to comply. Max stood and left.

Chapter 15

After spending the night at Orvan's cave, Seth, Rachel, and Galen joined the troll for breakfast. While Seth and Galen packed some provisions and prepared to leave, Rachel went to Orvan and unclasped the necklace that had saved her life. "This belongs to you," she told him.

"Keep it," he answered.

Rachel shook her head, "I couldn't. This was a gift from your love. I could never take it."

"You must keep it. Because the fairy dust is old and was not applied directly to your skin it is possible that if you take the necklace off than the acena virus will affect you again." He paused and then added, "She would have wanted you to have it."

"Oh Orvan...I don't know what to say."

"Rachel, if she had known that her fairy dust was going to save the life of the lady who imagined most of Xsardis, she would have leaped with joy. Please, keep it."

Rachel strung the vial back around her neck. "I can never thank you enough for all you've done."

"Ready to go?" Galen asked.

She nodded her head and they started out. At lunch Rachel noticed that they had only brought enough food for a few meals and asked Galen why.

He informed her, "By tomorrow afternoon we will reach the fields of Valinor and will have no need for food or water."

"The fields of Valinor?" Rachel questioned, and then her memory started to come back. "Oh, yes, I remember now. The fields of Valinor—home of the Valinor fruit trees. Their fruit comes in different colors but it is all sweet and refreshing. There is also a stream that runs throughout the land and the water there is the purest in all Issym."

"Correct," Galen told her.

"The Valinor trees are enchanted," Seth added. "Neither rain nor shine nor lack of either affects them. Their bark is some of the sturdiest known."

"Correct again," Galen smiled. "And you two thought you didn't remember anything about this world."

"Nothing of value," Rachel answered.

"Not yet, but the longer you stay here, the more you will recall. Why won't you help us?"

"I have a responsibility to see that Mary and Elise, the two twins who came here with me, get home safely," Rachel replied. "Besides, we've told you, we can't help."

"We just want to go home," Seth added.

Everyone was silent for a while. After they had finished eating, Galen stood up. "Come on," he encouraged. "We've got a long distance to travel."

As they walked, Galen once again tried to convince Seth and Rachel to help Issym. "You imagined everything about Xsardis. You can do more than you think in the fight against Smolden." But the teens remained firm—they were convinced that they could not help, and focused on getting back to Earth.

Galen decided to make an extra stop. *They need to see how evil Smolden is and what they can do with God on their side against the powers of evil.*

It was raining that night as Galen led Seth and Rachel to a town, which was surrounded by a large, wooden gate. Galen pulled his cloak over his face and knocked. "Who is it?" questioned a voice.

"Three weary travelers," Galen replied. They were admitted, and Galen led Seth and Rachel toward a building on the far side of the town. Hoping for an inn with a comfortable bed, Rachel was disappointed to see shelves full of books. *Why has Galen brought us to a library?* Rachel asked herself.

They sat down on the benches near a blazing fireplace. Rachel and Seth took off their cloaks and set them out to dry before the fire, but Galen left his on, keeping its hood close to his face. Rachel looked around her and saw that there was only one floor to the building, but it held multitudes of books. A woman came over, carrying three hot drinks. They each took one and she promised to return with a warm meal.

As she stepped away, Galen softly spoke to Seth and Rachel, "I have brought you here for a reason. This is my home, Fort Misson—the fort I will someday rule. This library is very special. It contains the most history ever found in one place on Issym.

"You see, years ago on Asandra there lived a man named Joppa. He recorded history. His work was made up mostly of Asandra's past, but every other year, someone from Issym would take vast amounts of knowledge and reports to Asandra, where Joppa would compile all the information into a clearly written record. He would make two copies of this work and would give one of them to the next person to come from Issym.

"Some of the texts were lost, but most can be found here. If you are looking for Issym's history, this is the place to come."

"Why are we looking for history?" Seth inquired, who had never liked history, but on this dreary night was especially disinterested and grumpy.

"Because you need to see the cruelty of Smolden. Perhaps then you will agree to help." Galen was up on his feet and pulling out books before Rachel or Seth could protest.

The woman who had brought them drinks came back over with three plates of turkey. "Your friend certainly seems to know his way around the library," she commented.

"Yes, he does," Seth replied, accepting the food.

Galen had allowed the hood of his cloak to fall back and the woman told Rachel and Seth, "He looks strangely familiar." She stared, trying to remember, and then declared, "Oh never mind," and went back to her business.

Galen returned to Seth and Rachel with several books. He handed one to each of them and began to speak, "These two books are full of the accounts of Smolden's actions." Rachel and Seth started to flip through them. "You will see that men, frogs, airsprites and mushnicks were enslaved and treated horribly. Anyone who resisted Smolden's reign was killed without mercy. You will read accounts of families torn apart, children orphaned, people starving and lives hardly worth living." He stopped talking as they took in a few pages.

Then Galen showed them another manuscript as he continued, "Part of this book contains an account of Smolden's first battle to take Issym. Our army outnumbered his, we were better equipped, and much more prepared, but he still won." Seth took the manuscript and both he and Rachel looked over it—the text was full of countless strategies used against Smolden, but not one of them had worked, mostly due to the fact that the dragon could not be hurt. His army had been mostly defeated but the dragon himself had lived on to torment the people of Issym.

Galen unrolled a scroll, "This is the account of the two of you climbing Mt. Smolden to retrieve the gem of light. With your help and God's blessing we stopped Smolden, but did not kill him. Now I am not saying that God can't defeat Smolden without you; He can do anything. But sometimes He uses people, like in the Bible story of Esther.

"Esther's people, the Jews, were going to be killed. She was the queen and knew that God wanted her to talk to the king so that he would save her people. But if Esther went before the king uncalled for she would face execution. So what did Esther do? She prayed and had her people pray. Then she trusted in God and went before the king.

"If she had not gone, God would have saved the Jews anyway. As her cousin told her, 'For if you remain silent at this time, relief and deliverance for the Jews will arise from another place, but you and your father's family will perish. And who knows but that you have come to royal position for such a time as this?' God wanted to use Esther, just as I believe He wants to use you."

Seth shifted uncomfortably as Galen continued, "All Queen Esther had to do was follow God's plan. When she did, God saved her and her family and her people. This isn't just a story—it really happened. Now it's your turn. Will you follow God's plan for you? Perhaps you have come to Issym for such a time as this.

"Maybe I'm wrong. If you tell me that fighting Smolden isn't what God wants from you, then I'll let it go. But I believe that God has brought you both here for a reason."

Overwhelmed, Rachel asked, "Why us?"

Galen replied, "Why Esther? Why was I called to wander? God's wisdom is beyond our understanding."

Galen handed them two ancient pages of writing. "These are some of the writings of Queen Asandra. They are the most valuable documents in this library. These pages tell the story of when Issym left the land he ruled to return to his former home to serve in battle. Do you think that he wanted to leave? Don't you think he would have rather stayed with his wife in a land of safety? But he had a calling and he had to follow."

"But Issym was a warrior," Seth protested. "We're just teenagers."

"A great man named Paul once wrote a letter to a young man named Timothy. Do you know what he said? 'Do not let anyone look down on you because you are young, but set an example for the believers in speech, in life, in love…'"

Rachel cut him off and finished what he was saying, "..in faith and in purity. 1st Timothy 4:12."

"The point is," Galen went on, "that even though Issym was a warrior, Esther was a queen and Timothy was a teenager, they still had to do things that were hard for them because it was the right thing to do. So, will you rise up to the occasion? Will you join Esther and Issym and Timothy in the ranks of heroes?"

Seth and Rachel took in the information. Neither one of them wanted to help; they were teenagers and had enough problems of their own without trying to save a world from an evil dragon. All they wanted to do was go home, spend time with their families, sleep in real beds, get on the internet, take showers, and so on. They did not think they could help. But they could not deny that they *should* help. The responsibility was unavoidable; they could no longer ignore the voice inside their hearts, the voice of the Holy Spirit, saying, *Help Issym. Don't be afraid. Your God is with you.*

Standing up, Seth said, "I'm in."

Galen stepped towards him and grasped his forearm, "Strength and honor, my brother."

Seth embraced Galen's forearm in return, "Strength and honor."

Rachel did not need to add her own agreement. She was sure they knew.

Their server came back over to take their plates. "Hey, I've figured it out! You're... you're Galen, Lord Asaph's son!"

"Yes, I am. Please, I don't wish for people to know that I am here," pleaded Galen, but it was too late; the woman had already run from the building. "Great," Galen sighed.

"Aren't you glad that you are home?" Rachel asked.

"Of course I am," Galen replied. "But I have tried to stay away from Fort Misson for a reason. I knew that if I came back, I would never want to leave again. Now, the whole town will know I'm here and come to see us, and I won't have the strength to go. Unless we get out of here, right now."

"Not so fast, Galen," a woman with a child cradled in her arms said as she stepped in the door. "My brother's been gone for three years, missed my wedding, missed the birth of my first child, and now is trying to leave before I see him. I don't think so."

"Seth and Rachel, I'd like you to meet my sister, Karen," Galen introduced as he hugged her. Then he told his sister, "I've got to get out of here before everyone sees me."

"You've been gone for so long Galen. Why must you leave?" Karen responded.

Asaph, Galen's father, was the next to appear. After him, people started to pour into the building and soon it was overflowing. Karen pulled Seth and Rachel outside and told them, "You'd probably like to get some rest. You can stay at my house. Follow me."

Early the next morning, while most of the town was asleep, Galen slipped out of his room and walked to one house in particular. Outside, a young woman was folding laundry. "You didn't come to see me last night," Galen commented.

"I figured that if you wanted to see me, you'd come here," the woman replied, without looking at him.

"I was afraid that you were…"

"Married?" she suggested. "No, Galen. I promised you when you first started talking about leaving Fort Misson to wander that I would wait for you. I still love you and I am still waiting. You said that you knew that God wanted you to go. How can I argue with God? Though I am still puzzled as to why He told you to wander. It seems to me that you would have more of a purpose here."

"I think I now know why. Andrea, I have missed you so. The only reason I never came back to see you is that I knew if I looked at you, I wouldn't have the strength to leave again, and I must not stay."

"Then why are you back?" she asked, turning now to face him. "And you said that you knew the reason that God told you to wander. What is it?"

"I brought with me Seth and Rachel, the two who imagined Issym. They needed to see some of the books from the library. I wanted to depart before anyone recognized me, but it didn't work out like that. I think that I was supposed to find those two and help them in their quest. I'm taking them to the land of the mushnicks and fairies."

"You should go before the fort wakes up. If you are not gone before breakfast, your father and sister and little brother won't let you leave all day," Andrea told him.

"I know. But, in your opinion, how is Preston doing?"

"Your little brother has grown to be quite the man. At first he couldn't understand why you left, but now he respects you for it."

"And Karen, how is she?"

Andrea smiled and threw a rag at him, "Galen, why are you stalling? Get out of here so that you can come back to me quicker."

He stepped towards her. "There's a war going on for Issym. Smolden is trying to take it again. Who knows what will happen? I may never see you again."

"Don't talk like that." She struggled to keep the color in her face.

"We need everyone we can get to help fight this battle. I have a letter for my father—to convince people to join our cause. Would you deliver it to him?"

"Of course."

"I should go." Galen tore himself away from her and woke up Seth and Rachel. They left Fort Misson before anyone else was awake.

A man snuck away from the underground. He started running back to Prince Aldair's castle. He was a new recruit—he had only been one of Smolden's soldiers for a few days but in those few days he had learned enough to be scared. In truth, this man was a spy sent from Princess Valerie, Prince Aldair's sister. He traveled back to the castle with all haste to report what he had learned.

Elise and Mary ran out of the room crying. "Get out!" Queen Danielle's screech echoed down the hallway after them. In reality it was not Danielle, but Sasha in the queen's form. The twins had come to bring the queen flowers but had accidentally knocked a glass of water onto Sasha's lap. Needless to say, the evil shape shifter was not happy.

That wasn't the only reason for Sasha's displeasure. Playing the part of the airsprites queen was not as painless as it looked. Everyone wanted to come in and talk to her, but whenever she tried to ask about the gem of light, the airsprites laughed nervously and wouldn't answer. *What is wrong with these sprites?* Sasha thought. *Couldn't they just tell me where the gem is? But no...they want me to be friendly with stupid little children and to entertain airsprite women! Is anything worth this?*

The shape shifter's frown lifted. Something was worth it. Rule of Issym was worth it. The secret of eternal youth that Smolden had promised to teach her was worth it. And eventually, when she discovered the dragon's weakness and killed him, this would be worth it.

Earlier than any of the other young shape shifters, Sasha had striven to develop her talents. She could shift into any form by the time she was ten, a feat which takes most shifters till they are thirty or even fifty. When she was twenty-one she could morph into different forms at the same time, something very few shifters have *ever* been able to achieve. The secret of eternal youth was her last and greatest challenge. Soon she would have achieved it. Sasha would have gained the abilities that the ancient shifters had possessed.

Her thoughts were interrupted by Jennet. She was the real Danielle's closest friend and had noticed the change in the attitude of the queen. "Danielle, can I talk to you for a moment?" she asked.

No, thought Sasha but she answered, "Yes."

"You seem different today," Jennet started. "Yelling at children and not wanting to talk to any of the ladies who have come to see you—I just don't understand."

"There's nothing wrong with me," Sasha snapped.

"Of course." Jennet started to leave but suggested, "Maybe you should take the day off."

Sasha opened her mouth to say no but thought better of it. In sweet tones the shape shifter told Jennet, "You know, I think that's a good idea."

Jennet smiled and left. Sasha mused, *With my free time, I'll search for the gem myself. And the sooner I find it, the sooner I can get away from these stupid, smiley airsprites!*

"Arvin, do you think that people are looking for you?" Max asked.

The prisoner looked up, aware of the strange tone in Max's voice. They had spent many hours together and Arvin thought he knew Max pretty well. "Yes."

"I'm sure no one's looking for me. They probably don't even know that I'm missing."

Taking a breath, Arvin asked, "By *they* you mean Seth and Rachel?" Max nodded and Arvin inquired, "Do you want to be rescued? Aren't you willingly helping Smolden?"

Max became defensive, "You make it sound like a bad thing!"

Arvin was silent. The teen squirmed in discomfort. He did not want the prisoner thinking badly of him, though why, he did not know. He tried to turn the topic back around, "I'm sure Seth isn't looking for me, but good! I wouldn't want his help, even if I was in trouble."

The prisoner shook his head.

"What?" Max spat, the anger inside him now turning on Arvin.

"Don't yell at me," Arvin ordered. "I'm not your enemy." The prisoner waited a second and then asked, "Max, do you want to leave the underground?"

"Things were really good when I got here, but honestly now, I wonder if Smolden will ever send me home."

"But do you want to go?"

"I..." Max paused, "should get back before someone realizes I'm missing."

Chapter 16

In the middle of the next day, Seth, Rachel, and Galen reached a hill looking down upon the fields of Valinor. For most of their journey they had traveled on an overgrown wood's road and had wearied of constantly being scraped and scratched by trees and bushes. Now as they looked down at the fields of Valinor, with the slim, curving river flowing through the land, the trees with colorful fruit calling to be picked, and the grass beckoning, "Come lie down on me and rest!" they were elated.

A group of trees created a glade on one side of the stream. Their bark was white and shimmering and their leaves were blue with a unique shape and texture. It appeared that a few of the trees had been carefully harvested and saplings had begun to sprout from the remaining trunk.

Past the grove, the sun shone brightly down upon the other trees and bright rays caused their fruit to let off extra shine. It was perfect, like a dream.

Though the three travelers were weary, nothing could keep them from racing down the hill. Their sole desire was to enter the fields of Valinor, eat a piece of fruit, drink some of the crystal clear water, and bask in the sun while lying in the grass.

"I could stay here for the rest of my life!" Rachel exclaimed, taking the first bite of a delicious piece of fruit.

"Me too," Seth agreed.

When they had all enjoyed an abundance of fruit and water, the sun was setting. Seth and Galen built a fire with the fallen branches from some of the trees. The Valinor wood seemed to let off extra heat. Seth figured that for the first time since he had arrived in Issym, the cold would not keep him awake.

"I'm surprised no one has built a house here," Rachel commented. All three of them were on their backs, looking up at the stars. "There's plenty of wood, food, and water, and it seems like it would make a good place to start a town."

"It is true that you would lack for nothing if you stayed here, but the fields of Valinor are not a home. It is good to take a vacation every now and then but you must go back to your own people and fulfill your duties."

Galen sat up. Rachel and Seth followed suit. "We each have our mission in life," the wanderer continued. "The thing about this place is that no matter who you are you *can't* fulfill your mission here. It's impossible. It has to do with the enchantment of the place.

"Here is where you get restored so that you have the strength to carry on your tasks, but it is not where you do them," Galen finished.

A tiny bit of sadness crept into Seth's heart as he remembered that the next day they would have to leave the fields behind and go back to their mission of trying to retrieve a glowing orb from an evil dragon. He tried to forget those feelings. "What I can't figure is why 'bad guys' don't make the fields their home. I mean, they don't care what their mission is, or whether or not they fulfill it. Plus, I've been to Mt. Smolden (or at least, I imagined climbing it once or twice) and it is cold and barren. Why would anyone choose Mt. Smolden over Valinor?"

"'Bad guys' hate this place. I think it has something to do with the blessing given to Valinor."

"*The blessing*?" Rachel inquired.

"It is written in a book in the library at Fort Misson that when God created Xsardis He blessed these fields. He made them a haven for all who believe in Him. God made it so that the trees would always thrive, the river would always be deep, and the grass would always be green.

"Bad guys hate this place because it was blessed by God. They try to say He doesn't exist so they can't acknowledge that this exists. They hate anything that has to do with Him.

"I see," said Seth.

Rachel yawned. The day had been relaxing and it would be nice to sleep in the peace of Valinor. She felt safe for the first time since they had been forced into Xsardis.

"We should get some sleep," Galen announced. "Tomorrow, we continue on your quest for the fairies and mushnicks."

There was something incredibly irritating about Arvin and the way he would just sit there and listen to whatever Max said, no matter how ridiculous it was. He would not say anything about what he thought, Arvin would just ask some small question in return. He implied his true feelings by what he didn't say. Why did Arvin have to make Max feel so guilty for talking badly about Seth, or helping Smolden? What did the guy want from him? Max made up his mind; he would not allow this prisoner to influence him any more.

And yet, as the teen stood in Smolden's lair there was a great discomfort. The dragon rasped a question that Max knew the answer to. This beast offered him riches and home. And yet, the prisoner who seemed to offer nothing held more sway. "I don't know," Max lied to the leviathan.

"Do you know anything?" the beast swatted at Max with a powerful hand.

The teen ducked, angry with Arvin because he could not be angry with himself. He left the dragon's lair and marched straight to Arvin's cell, ready to tell him off. This man had no right to be controlling his life so. But the second his eyes landed on the prisoner, his heart stopped. The man was laying down, color completely gone.

Was he even breathing? "Arvin!" He fell beside him and reached through the bars towards him. "Arvin..."

The man stirred at Max's touch. He slowly, and obviously with much difficultly sat up. "What is it?" Arvin asked; he hoped he had managed to hide the weakness in his voice.

"Are you alright?"

"Yes; just sleeping." His eyes fell closed and one breathless moment passed before they opened again.

"You're not okay. What's wrong?"

"Probably just hunger."

"When was the last time you ate?"

"I don't know, several days."

"Days! Why did you not tell me?"

"You've been complaining about your own food shortage."

"I'll go get you something."

"Max... I've been here many months," his words lacked their usual clarity.

"Yes, you have. I'll go get you something." Max knew nothing of health, but this man appeared to be in great danger.

"No! Stay. Listen." Arvin gripped Max's arm. "Smolden told me that I would have months of misery and then death, when his victory was near."

"Yes."

"Sometimes an undergrounder comes by my cell; I have overheard them talking. They say that Smolden will soon take his army aboveground. The dragon will not leave me here alive."

"What are you saying?"

"My time is almost up." Max had no words. "But you... your time just beginning."

"I'm not so sure about that. He's pretty angry at me."

"You don't help him?"

"No. Thanks to you I apparently now have a conscience."

The prisoner laughed. "You'll need more than that. Only for so long can you claim neither to serve Smolden nor God. A choice must be made."

"Allow me to get you food. This conversation can wait."

"No." But Max was already gone.

Max hurried back to Arvin carrying a plate of dry bread and a small piece of chicken, along with a skin of water. The prisoner gratefully accepted the food.

"There is something different about you than most people," Max commented. "Anyone else would have used me to get them food the very first time we met; but you didn't say anything. And, you disapprove of everything I do and yet, you still are very kind to me."

"I could tell you how I became different."

"Could I learn it?" Max was not certain if he really want to learn it, but he had to know more. It was like this prisoner held water for his parched heart.

"Oh yes, I am sure of that."

"Tell me."

"There is a man to whom you must go. He will help and guide you to be a good man and to make right decisions."

"Where is he?"

"Long ago, He lived and then was murdered."

"Then how did you learn from Him?" asked Max.

"He came back to life."

"What?" Max questioned, not expecting that twist.

"You see, He died for my sins and your sins and for everyone's sins and after three days came back to life."

"Oh yeah, I know that story. The crazy people on my world think that it's true," grunted Max, rolling his eyes. "Come on, you don't actually believe that stuff, do you?"

"Max, you asked me what was different about me and that is my answer to you. Who I am is no one special but through Christ's strength I can be different from the world, which is why you like spending time with me."

Max tried not to look at Arvin. He knew what he could expect —a judgmental face and eyes full of condemnation, That's what his uncle had been like when he had 'witnessed' to him. Seth had never been like that when he talked about God, but Max was still sure that when he turned to face Arvin he would see stern eyes. The teen looked toward the prisoner, but to his surprise, Arvin's face was once again full of compassion.

Max needed time to think. He turned his attention to the wall and started picking at it. A brick came lose. Max reached his hand into the hole were the brick had been; he pulled out a piece of leather. A gold medallion and a key were attached to it. There were some runes etched into its surface and it had a hole in it for the key. Max showed it to Arvin. "Insert the key," the prisoner told him. Arvin's voice had changed; he sounded edgy and tense.

"Why?" Max inquired.

"Lad, if you consider me a friend you will do it, for it may be my way to escape."

"How will it help you escape?" asked Max, feeling good to have some control over Arvin.

"Smolden has long searched for the medallion and key you have in your hand. I had no idea that it was hidden here. In fact it is possible that no one knew where it was."

"Why would he search for it?" Max questioned, realizing the power he held in his hand. If he delivered it to Smolden he would be treated like a prince again—maybe he could even go home like the dragon had promised. If he inserted the key he could save Arvin and escape with the prisoner from the underground. Once he rejoined Seth, maybe the two of them could go home.

"Because…" Arvin was cut off by the sounds of hollering and shouting coming not from the corridor but from one of the main rooms of the underground. Someone was hollering Max's name.

Arvin told him, "They're looking for you. Quickly either insert the key or put it back where it came from but don't give it to Smolden and don't let them find you here."

Max thought about it for a second. He was not ready to make up his mind on what to do with the medallion and key, so in a moment of utter selfishness, he pocketed the device and scampered out the door.

He slipped into the room where a large crowd had gathered. Minotaurs stood on the right side, and humans and toads on the left. Kerub, Smolden's right hand minotaur, stood in the middle, shoulders hunched and ax drawn. He had his foot on the chest of a human, who looked helpless and small compared to the creature. The humans to his left looked ready to fight, but this did nothing to make the man on the ground feel secure. The crowds were noisy, some creatures grunting their battle calls, others hollering insults, still others simply shouting because they could. Kerub's voice boomed out toward the human on the ground as he brandished his weapon, "You were supposed to keep an eye on him! Where is Max?"

"I don't know," the man whimpered, knowing the wrath of the minatour was about to kill him.

"I'm right here," shouted the teen. He had spoken just in time to save the poor soldier's life.

Kerub moved towards Max and grabbed him by his shirt collar. "Smolden wants to see you." He turned towards the human on the ground, "I'll deal with you later. And the rest of you, get back to your business."

Inside the dragon's lair, Max felt more uncomfortable than ever before. "Max," rasped Smolden, "you haven't been of much help to me. I have opened my home to you and made you a prince but you won't answer any of my questions." Max didn't like where the conversation was going.

"Now, it won't be long before my troops go above ground and I need you to do something for me. I have in my possession a way for you to go home," lied the dragon. "It is one of Universe Girl's orbs." Max's eyes lit up. He had heard Flibbert talking about the spheres.

"However, I am not just going to give it to you, since you've been of so little help. You must find Seth and Rachel and bring them here. Then I will send you all home."

"Why would you help us?" Max was questioning.

"Seth and Rachel are deluded into helping the people of Issym fight against me. They are causing me more harm than good. I'd like to get rid of you all, if you won't help me."

It made sense to Max. That night as he lay on his cot he thought things over. *If what Arvin has been saying is true then Smolden can't really want to send Seth, Rachel, and I home. If I bring Seth and Rachel to the underground Smolden might kill all of us; if I don't do it,*

Smolden might kill me. If I put the key into the medallion who knows what will happen? Somebody help me!

He heard a voice inside him say, *I can help you. You know I can.*

Max tried to tune it out. *I'll be fine on my own,* he thought.

You need my help and all you have to do is ask.

Max knew who the voice was. It was the voice of God knocking on his heart's door. Arvin's words about Jesus had sunk into his very soul, and he longed for the peace that poor prisoner had. Max had seen the lives of Seth and Arvin and how much happier they were than he was—even if one of them was sitting in a prison cell.

But Max was stubborn. *When I want Your help I'll ask for it.* With that he rolled over and went to sleep.

Chapter 17

Early the next morning, Max slipped into Arvin's jail cell. "Hello."

The prisoner didn't say a word. *He must be mad at me for not inserting the key into the medallion,* Max thought. He told the prisoner, "I didn't give the medallion to Smolden."

"Good," Arvin replied.

There were a few moments of silence. Max told him, "Smolden's sending me on a journey today to find Seth and Rachel. He says that if I bring them here, he'll send us all home."

Arvin was clearly disappointed, "You can't really believe that."

"I have a plan to ensure the dragon keeps his word."

"And what is that?"

"I won't tell him I have the medallion until I get back with Seth and Rachel. I won't let him have it unless he sends us home."

"You wouldn't!"

"I have to. You can't understand."

"I can't understand wanting to go home? Max, my greatest wish in the world is to go home; but you can't betray Issym like that! And you can't betray Seth and Rachel."

"How am I betraying them? I'm helping them."

"You must know that Smolden will kill them if he gets them into the underground."

"Why should I believe you? You're the one behind bars."

"Oh Max..." Arvin shook his head. As far as he could tell, the battle had been fought for Max's soul and it had been lost.

"There you are, criticizing *me*, witnessing to *me*, telling *me* that I need God. Well I don't. I'll find my own way home without Him, you'll see! You've treated me like a child, but I can take care of myself. And what about you? You can't be perfect; after all, you're a prisoner."

"I'm not perfect, far from it, but..."

Max could hear the sound of a door swinging open. Arvin's face was drained of all color. The teen looked behind him. Smolden's head minotaur, Kerub, barged into the room. There were two humans with him. When Kerub saw Max he growled, "What are you doing here?"

"I... ah..." Max stammered. He saw the two humans unlocking Arvin's cell. "What do you want with him?"

"Lord Smolden has sentenced him to death," Kerub answered him. "Now, tell me what you are doing here."

Max did not say a word. Kerub ordered, "Get out! If you see that guard of yours tell him that he is as good as dead!"

Max scurried through the door, but he stayed just outside the room. He watched as the two humans dragged Arvin to his feet and pulled him out of his cell into the room Max had just left. Kerub gripped his ax, ready to be Arvin's executioner.

Max knew that if he did not act, the prisoner would be killed. He could not let that happen. *Why?* Max asked himself, *Why am I so worried about his life? If I help him, Smolden will kill me. Why am I willing to risk my life to save his?*

He answered himself, *Because he is my friend and a noble man—a man with Jesus in his heart. I fully believe that Jesus is what makes him and Seth so different. Jesus died for my sin and for some strange reason God loves me. God is the only one who can save me. I pray that He will help me here and now.*

Were these really his thoughts? They raced through his mind in a matter of seconds. What had happened to the doubt he had always carried within him about everything? Was he really ready to put his whole trust into Someone?

Lord Jesus, he prayed, knowing that he would die for what he was about to do. *My life is in your hands.* He reached into his pocket and pulled out the medallion. He tried to put the key in but dropped the piece of leather, with the medallion and the key, to the ground. Max dove after them.

Kneeling in the dirt he desperately tried to get the key in the hole. He glanced into the other room. Kerub was about to strike Arvin down. Was he too late?

He managed to get the key in. Nothing happened. Kerub began to bring his ax forward. Max tried turning the key. It moved one full rotation.

Flibbert knew he should leave the village of Prince Edgar but he was determined to get somefrog in the village to aid the cause of Issym. Though the village frogs pretended to ignore him, Flibbert had a gut feeling that some of them wanted to help. Throughout the day he continued to try to persuade them to go to Prince Aldair's castle.

As night fell, Flibbert was encouraged, seeing one young frog kiss his wife goodbye. The frog nodded at Flibbert in a way that said, "I'm joining your cause," and slipped out of the village without anyone else seeing him. At least Flibbert had raised one supporter.

Finally, as darkness fell, Prince Edgar came out again and shouted "I grow weary of hearing your wails. Arrest this frog!"

Flibbert was dragged from the village and taken to a building made of iron. As he was thrown into a prison cell, Flibbert noted that there was only one other frog held captive. The jail keeper declared as he locked Flibbert's cell, "By order of Prince Edgar, you will stay here without food or water for the rest of your days, however short they may be."

Sleeping frogs and humans could be found everywhere in Prince Aldair's castle, because by now the frogs and humans of several villages had started to arrive. They had explained to Princess Valerie, Aldair's sister who was ruling until her brother returned, why they had come, and she had welcomed them with open arms.

Curt, who was the captain of the guard, together with Princess Valerie and a few others, stood in the throne room rubbing the sleep out of their eyes. The sun had not yet risen and the room was dimly lit by a few torches on the walls. These men and women had been woken up to hear the story of a man who had just arrived. "After you asked me to spy in the underground, I went there straight away. After a few days I overheard a conversation between the shape shifter Sasha and Smolden," the man said. Everyone in the room was familiar with Sasha —her evil deeds preceded her—and who didn't know of Smolden and his cruelty?

"I decided I should come back and tell you," the man continued. His clothes were worn and his face was scruffy and dirty. He had obviously wasted no time on hygiene while in the underground. "On my way here, a fairy man of the green descended before me, and when he found out what I had learned, he flew me here so that I could inform you more quickly."

"What did you learn?" Curt questioned, his senses now fully alert, despite the early hour.

"Sasha is going to go to the airsprites and try to steal the gem of light. She's probably there right now."

"What?" asked Princess Valerie, very much alarmed at this news. The gem of light was all that they had for protection against Smolden. Valerie could think of no two worse enemies than Smolden and Sasha; if they were really working together... She shuddered.

"It's true your highness," the man repeated. "I'm sure of it."

"But we have heard nothing of this from any airsprites! She has not attacked them."

"It is possible," Curt surmised, "that Sasha has taken on the form of an airsprite to search for the gem, and as such would go unnoticed."

"Thank you," she told the man who had brought the information. "You were right to hurry back with this news. Return to your family and take your much deserved rest."

The man withdrew from the throne room, as did everyone else except Princess Valerie and Curt. "Why didn't we see this coming? It seems so obvious now," she remarked, moving towards a window and looking out at the houses and the tents set up below.

"No one but a shape shifter can enter airsprites territory unless they go through Flibbert the guardfrog's house. And if they did that, they would be detected by one of the guards. We knew shape shifters were dangerous, but we thought we had them well enough contained. And your brother and I believed Sasha too prideful to work for Smolden, so we never foresaw this. The dragon and shape shifter have created a simple, but brilliant plan. They attack our trust. We were foolish to give it."

"Any good side to this?" she asked, resting her head in her hands. Valerie did not feel prepared enough to rule. *Just a few more years and I would have been ready,* she thought. Now she wished terribly that someone else would take her crown.

"At least we know now what Smolden's plans are."

The sun had begun to rise, and one ray landed on the portrait of Prince Aldair, hanging on the far wall of the throne room. "I wish my brother were here. He would know what to do." She prepared herself to ask the question to which she already knew the answer, "Is there any news of him?"

"No," Curt shook his head. "Your brother's visit to Prince Edgar was investigated, but none of the townsfrogs were willing to speak with my men."

Just then a man burst into the room. As he tried to bow the momentum of his steps made him tumble to the ground.   "Sorry to intrude," he panted quickly as he regained his footing, "but there are shape shifters in the castle and they are asking to speak to you!"

"What?" *Shape shifters, in the castle? How did they get in? Why have they come?* Valerie's mind was filled with questions. "Could things get any worse?"

"It may not be as bad as it seems," the captain of the guard answered. "They would not risk coming to a place filled with frog stones unless they had something important to say." He ordered the man, "Send them in but I want ten frogs, wearing armor, up here immediately." He turned towards the princess. "We will be completely safe. The stones of the frog's armor keep shifters from being able to change their form, so they can be killed. They will not risk their lives by attacking us."

The frogs entered the throne room mere moments before the shape shifters. Princess Valerie tried to put on her most stately manor. She sat erect in her chair, hiding her troubled face under a mask of calm.

When the shape shifters appeared, they were all in human form. They bowed before Princess Valerie and one, who appeared to be the leader, handed a letter to her.

Valerie read it over and gave it to Curt. "That is Universe Girl's signature and the mark of her signant ring," she announced.

The lead shifter told them, "My name is Kate, and we want to help."

Seth and Rachel were glad to have Galen as a guide, a protector and a companion as they traveled along the road. Rain had been pouring down since they left the fields of Valinor and a certain feeling of gloominess had overtaken Seth and Rachel, but Galen appeared to be ever cheerful.

On the third day since they had left the fields, the sun finally appeared. As Galen played cheerful tunes upon his flute, his companions' spirits began to rise.

They ate the last of the fruit from Valinor for lunch. Even though it was all they had eaten for three days, none of them were tired of it. The fruit was perfectly juicy and sweet and there was nothing tastier on Issym or, for that matter, Earth.

"You can't even feel guilty about eating this fruit," Rachel commented as she finished off a piece, "like with chocolate. Chocolate tastes wonderful but if you eat too much it will make you sick. This stuff is actually good for you."

And it was true. The fruit did make one stronger and healthier. The three companions had been walking faster and taking fewer breaks as they traveled because of the fruit.

About midday the ground suddenly trembled and shook. All of Issym swayed, trees crashed to the ground, and a great chasm opened up in the center of the continent, dividing it almost completely.

Seth and Galen fell to the ground. It was a miracle neither of them were injured as the quaking continued. It was half an hour before the tremors ceased. As Seth and Galen regained their feet, their ears were ringing and they knew they would be sore for several days, but they had no serious injuries.

They walked over to the chasm that had formed in the middle of Issym. The opening was over a mile wide!

"What could have caused such an earthquake?" Galen muttered.

Seth was puzzled. He had very limited knowledge of earthquakes, but what he knew of them said that it should not have been possible for an earthquake to last so long or to have created such a chasm. When he was a kid he had pretended there could have been such an earthquake...

An image of a gold medallion and a key popped into Seth's head and he knew that he was remembering something he had once imagined. He thought hard, trying to bring back this memory. He recalled an old fairy man lying on the ground, wounded from a battle. He was about to die and handed a medallion and key to Seth as he commanded, "Keep the medallion safe. It will cause untold destruction. It will divide the land."

Could the medallion have been the cause of the earthquake? When the old fairy had said, "It will divide the land," had he been speaking literally?

Seth's thoughts were interrupted when Galen asked, "Do you see Rachel?"

They looked around them. Galen pointed to the other side of the opening the earthquake had caused. A figure was lying on the ground.

"Great," Seth rolled his eyes. "How on Xsardis are we supposed to get to her?"

A few minutes time revealed a greater problem—Rachel was not getting up. "She must be hurt," Galen gravely declared.

"We have to get over there!" Seth cried.

Chapter 18

Rachel felt a hole opening between her feet and she leaped to her right. She hit her head on a boulder and fell to the ground, unconscious.

The wound should have killed her, but the necklace that Orvan had given her healed more than the acena virus. The fairy dust started to heal her concussion.

Rachel woke up a little less than an hour later. The quaking had stopped and she slowly sat up. She looked for Seth and Galen and spotted them across the chasm. She rolled her eyes. *Oh great!*

Seth saw Rachel stand up and shouted for joy. He called to her but the distance between them was too great for her to hear him. "What do we do now?" Seth asked Galen.

I suggest we proceed to the fairies," Galen answered. "Perhaps we can find a way to get her to walk with us, just on the other side of the chasm."

"What do you mean?"

"We both head the same direction, but you and I walk to the left of the gap and she walks to the right. Farther down the road the chasm may be small enough for us to rejoin her."

"Are you crazy?" exclaimed Seth. "We can't just leave her to walk over there by herself. Who knows what dangers she'll face! In case you haven't noticed, Smolden has been searching for us and if he finds her…"

"What do you want me to do, Seth?" Galen's raised voice interrupted the teen. "There is no crossing here. We must go on."

Seth had to admit that Galen had suggested the only plausible course of action. "Fine," he agreed with frustration, but not spite, in his voice.

They started walking north. Rachel saw them go and decided to follow. At first it was hard to keep the pace since her head was still healing, but the longer they walked the healthier she felt.

When Flibbert was thrown into his jail cell there was only one other frog in the prison, and his cell was directly across from Flibbert's own. "What did you do to get Prince Edgar mad at you?" Flibbert had asked him.

"I mentioned to one of my friends that I thought Prince Edgar was the worst frog ruler ever," the frog had replied. "I didn't think my friend would go and tell the prince."

"I'm Flibbert."

"Name's Daniel."

Flibbert was glad to know that someone else was willing to stand against Prince Edgar, and glad to think that he would have company until he died of starvation. A day later, however, Daniel called a guard and told him, "I'll do what Prince Edgar asked. I'll tell everyone that I was just being stupid and that Prince Edgar is a great ruler. And then I'll pledge my life to his service. But please, let me out!" So Daniel was released and Flibbert was alone in the jail. Maybe no one had the courage to stand up to Edgar after all.

On the morning of his second day in prison Flibbert was really beginning to wish he had paid more attention to eating while he had had the chance. While he had been traveling, food had seemed a hindrance, but now... what he wouldn't give for a piece of bread.

What was that noise? Flibbert looked out through the barred window of his cell. Flies, lots of flies, were swarming something. It didn't matter what. God had just given him dinner.

He shot his tongue through the bars and swallowed the first fly. Then he snapped his tongue out for another and another and another, until none were left.

He had just finished his meal when the ground began to rumble and shake. Suddenly the building fell to pieces around him. Part of the roof crashed onto Flibbert's leg and pinned him to the ground. He squeezed up the rest of him into as small a ball as he could manage and remained there as the earthquake continued and more of the building's pieces fell down around him.

When the quake ceased, he tried to get the piece of roof off his leg, but it wouldn't budge. Gashes covered his body and a deep wound in his arm gushed blood. The frog's strength was waning. He fought the slumber that threatened to take him and cried out to God for help. Finally the pain forced his eyes shut and he fell into a fitful, fevered slumber.

Princess Valerie had ordered that a breakfast table be set up for herself, Curt, Kate and her group of shape shifters. "We have broken off from the other shifters," Kate informed the princess and her captain of the army between bites of her breakfast. "We want to help you."

It was hard for Valerie and Curt to believe that a band of shape shifters could really be on the side of justice, but Valerie accepted it because of Universe Girl's recommendation.

"What can we do to assist you?" Kate inquired.

Princess Valerie thought about it for a second and then replied, "Actually, you have just solved a big problem for us. The shape shifter Sasha has gone to the land of the airsprites and is trying to steal the gem of light. We think she has taken on an airsprites form but we have no idea how to stop her. She could be any airsprites. If she steals the gem of light, Smolden will have an easy victory. We can't let her succeed. Perhaps you will be able to discern who Sasha is impersonating. Are you willing?

"I am. May I have a moment to discuss it with the rest of my people?"

"Of course." Princess Valerie and Curt rose and left the room.

"What do you think?" Kate asked the shape shifters.

"We came here to help and that is what we should do," replied one shifter and the others nodded their agreement.

They departed at once, heading away from the castle. Once they had put enough distance between themselves and the palace so that the frogs' stone armor had no effect on them, they took on the form of birds and flew to the clouds. Just as they arrived an earthquake shook the foundations of Issym.

As the earthquake rumbled in Smolden's domain, the men who had been holding Arvin fell to the ground along with the minotaur that had been about to chop off the prisoner's head. Arvin pushed himself up from the floor, rushed towards Max, and shouted, "Follow me." They dodged panicking humans, running minotaurs and hopping toads as they searched for an exit, any exit.

The ceiling was collapsing along with the walls and floor. Arvin knew they did not have much time to get out of the underground; they had to run as quickly as they could. But he had been cooped up in a jail cell, starved and beaten for months; his strength was low. Every move he made caused a new pain to rush up his body.

Arvin and Max scaled a steep floor and dived onto the grassy land of Issym. Things aboveground were not much better than below. A whole was opening up in the middle of Issym and threatened to swallow everyone around them. Max and Arvin ran from chasm.

When Arvin could go no farther the two fell panting to the ground and covered their heads as the quake continued. When it ceased there were a few moments of silence. Then Arvin exclaimed a breathless, "Thank you, Max."

Max told him, "Just before I tried to use the medallion, I asked Jesus to be my Savior. You could have told me, though, that an earthquake would erupt when I turned the key."

"You're right, I probably should have told you that," he laughed. "But the truth is that I didn't actually know that this was going to happen." He drew in a breath of free air.

"So where do we go from here?"

"North," he answered. "We'll head to... Prince Aldair's castle and see what we can find out."

Chapter 19

When Flibbert awoke, he was lying on a wooden table. He slowly sat up, eyes still closed. When he opened his eyelids he saw faces painted with vibrant colors and hair dyed fluorescently bright. The faces were only inches from his own. Flibbert jumped off the table and started to back away from the four plump, three-foot tall men with the brightly colored faces, white skin and flaming hair, but as he moved away the men moved closer.

"You're awake," exclaimed the one to Flibbert's left, whose face and whole body appeared to be painted purple with yellow circles, and whose bright green hair was sticking straight up. "My name is Cobby." He spoke without drawing a breath.

"I'm Freddy," rapidly said the one whose skin had purple triangles painted on top of white paint and whose hair was brilliant white.

The man with a blue body, red paint on his chin and the top of his forehead, and curly fluorescent red hair declared, "I'm Clarence."

The last man's face was painted lime green and had six vertical orange lines on it. "And I'm Simmy," he introduced himself. Flibbert couldn't help laughing inwardly at how strange they all looked —especially Simmy with his multicolored hair, which was sticking out in every direction.

Flibbert glanced quickly around the room, trying to figure out where he was. The frog saw furniture and cabinets and doors leading to other rooms. A fire blazed in a brick fireplace behind him.

"Are you feeling better?" Clarence inquired.

Flibbert instinctively examined his leg, knowing that he should feel the most pain there. It had been crushed in the earthquake, but he saw only a small scar. "How in Xsardis..." he muttered.

"You were almost dead when we found you," announced Simmy, pointing to Flibbert as he spoke.

"You must have gotten hurt in the *big* earthquake," put in Freddy as he opened his arms up wide to represent it.

"But how was I healed?" questioned Flibbert.

"Our fairy mended your leg," Clarence answered, gesturing toward the frog's appendage.

"Your fairy? What are you?" Flibbert inquired.

"We are mushnicks!" they answered in unison. Then they burst into song as they danced in circles around him,

Long ago the mushnicks
Made a pact with fairies
That if they would help Issym
We would always serve them.

Kindly fairies helped us
But didn't ask for anything.
We will always serve them
Anyways
Anyways

Because we love the fairies,
Yes, we love the fairies.
How we love the fairies,
Always.

Flibbert's head was ringing and he wished they would talk more quietly. *Well they certainly are a cheerful bunch. A little odd—but nice all the* same, he thought. *Since they are mushnicks it makes sense that their skin appears to have been painted, but they must actually have been born looking like that.*

"What did you think we were?" Cobby asked, laughing.

"I've never seen a mushnick before," replied Flibbert. The mushnicks and the fairies rarely left their home near Kembar plains, and Flibbert had not journeyed that far north.

"Never seen a mushnick!" exclaimed Clarence.

"You at least must have heard of us," Freddy chimed in, pointing to himself.

"Because if you haven't there are 148 more verses that tell about our history," Clarence told Flibbert, leaning in close to the frog.

"You've heard three but we would love to sing you more," offered Simmy.

"No," replied Flibbert, quickly and definitely. Though he enjoyed their company, he wanted to get moving. "I should be going."

The mushnicks' happy faces turned sad, and they looked as if they were going to cry. "Go?" Freddy sniffed. "Go where?"

Flibbert replied, "I have to go to frog villages and warn them about a coming battle. Is there a fairy around I could speak with?"

"The only fairy who lives here," Simmy answered as he pointed to the floor, "is Lady Esther and she is out." He pointed to the door. Flibbert noticed that everything the mushnicks said was accompanied by hand gestures and that the four little men never seemed to stop moving for even a second.

Flibbert was puzzled. He figured that since he was with mushnicks he was in the land of the fairies near Kembar plains. "But aren't we in the land of the mushnicks and fairies?" he asked.

"No," Freddy shook his head. "Almost all the fairies live there, but some don't. A few fairies are spread out over Xsardis."

Cobby told him, "Esther is one of those fairies."

"And we are her helpers," Clarence added.

Just then the door opened and Flibbert, for the first time in his life, saw a fairy. Her dress was floor length and white, a standard dress for fairy women, and the sparkles on her eyes and wings were blue, and formed beautiful spirals.

"Good to see you awake, Flibbert," the fairy greeted.

"How do you know me?" the frog inquired.

"I'm a fairy. I know many things, including your quest." Esther came in, closing the door behind her. "I want to thank you for helping to raise an army to defend the fairies and the mushnicks. We are eternally in your debt."

The fairy gracefully walked over to the fireplace and sat down on one of the two stools in front of it. She offered the other seat to Flibbert. "I and my people are grateful for your hard work gathering men and frogs, but we now have another task for you."

The mushnicks stood behind the fairy and the frog, leaning their faces in. Flibbert did not know whether to be amused by the creatures or annoyed.

"Your friend Seth and his traveling companion, Galen, have been separated from the Lady Rachel. She is on the other side of a chasm caused by the earthquake. They could not cross to her and decided to walk on. Now Rachel is heading straight for shape shifter territory.

"The chasm was at its widest were they were separated, but it will get narrower as they walk toward the Kembar plains. I hope that Seth and Galen will be able to cross to Rachel before the shape shifters catch her, but we cannot count on that. Help is on the way, just in case. I have spoken with Princess Valerie, and she has already sent the frogs that were at her castle to meet with Seth and Galen."

Why didn't Esther just go rescue Rachel herself? Flibbert thought. He did not ponder this very long, though, for no one had ever been able to understand fairies' strange strategies. "But what do you want from me?" asked Flibbert.

"I need you to go on and meet them."

Flibbert shook his head, thinking of his own quest. "What good will I be to Seth and Rachel anyway?"

"Once the army meets up with them it will easy for someone in that group to kidnap Seth and Rachel and take them to Smolden. We can't let that happen."

Flibbert rose from his chair. He would not hear even a fairy speak of good men and frogs as kidnappers, "You dishonor us with this talk."

Esther, still seated, looked him in the eye, "Times are hard, and we cannot deceive ourselves into believing that everyone is honorable. If someone were to turn Seth and Rachel over to Smolden, they would receive a king's wages. These two must be protected at all costs. They could be the key to defeating Smolden. I need you to take them away from the group and make sure they get to my fellow fairies and mushnicks safely."

"I have other work to do. Already I have wasted too much time. We need more men and frogs for the army. Why don't you go to Seth and Rachel?" Flibbert protested.

The mushnicks were as still as could be and the smiles had dropped off their faces. They never questioned their fairy's orders and now Flibbert was fighting with her. Stress permeated the room and the mushnicks squirmed in its presence.

"A fairy council has been called and I must attend," Esther responded. "And Seth and Rachel trust you, Flibbert. They'll listen to you and travel with you—they wouldn't do the same with me."

"You said that a man named Galen accompanied them—speak with him and get him to take them away from the army," Flibbert argued.

"We don't know Galen like we know you. We know *you* can be trusted, but Galen we're just not sure about."

"But I've never even met a fairy before," the frog protested, "how can you know me?"

Esther answered, "We've spoken with the airsprites and they trust you. Anyway, your deeds precede you—everyone knows what side you are on.

"But Galen?" she continued. "He's a wanderer—who just happened to bump into Seth and Rachel? It makes one think. Could he be working for Smolden? Could he be waiting for just the right opportunity to take Seth and Rachel? Or could he be a spy trying to learn our plans? No, we can't trust Galen with two people so vitally import to saving Issym. It has to be you who bring them to the fairies and mushnicks."

Esther's reasoning was sound, but Flibbert still had one problem. "Who will finish my previous quest?"

Smiles came back to the mushnicks faces as they all jumped up and down, shouting, "We'll go!"

Esther smiled and put her hand on Simmy's colorful head. She told her mushnicks, "Today you have made me ever so proud of you." They glowed under her praise.

Flibbert nodded his head, "I will go and retrieve Seth and Rachel, if the mushnicks will finish my quest."

"Rest here tonight," Esther told him, "and at first light you shall depart."

Chapter 20

Rachel was not very happy. For about two days she had been able to see Seth and Galen walking on the other side of the chasm, but now she had lost sight of them. She was tired and cranky and wasn't sure at what pace she should walk.

The earthquake had caused more damage than just one large chasm. Trees had come crashing down; holes and hills had developed. It was a long and difficult process to try to walk beside or climb over the holes, hills, and trees. Exhausted and hungry, Rachel sat down on one of the fallen limbs.

Why do I have all bad luck? she asked herself. *Why did I end up in Issym? Why did the acena virus attack me? Why was I separated from Seth and Galen? Why does everything bad that happens seem happen to me?*

Count your blessings, said the voice of God inside her.

What blessings? she retorted.

By coming to Issym, you were reacquainted with Seth, and you met honorable and good people like Galen, Flibbert and Ethelwyn, the Holy Spirit replied. *Orvan gave you his most treasured possession to save you from the acena virus. The earthquake could have killed you, but you're alive. You've been able to find enough food and water for the past two days. The list goes on and on. Besides, is being separated from Seth and Galen really that bad?*

As Rachel started to count her blessings her spirits revived. She stood up, ready to continue walking.

Suddenly a few trees transformed into three frogs and two humans with swords in hand. Rachel could not believe her eyes. The frogs and humans had most certainly not been around a second ago. Where could they have come from? *Shape shifters!* she thought. *Well, I can hope that they are friendly.* She tried to be optimistic but she could not remember imagining any shifters that were not evil. "Hello," she greeted as she swallowed her fear.

A frog moved around behind her and put his sword to her back. "Come with us," he commanded. Rachel complied. What else could she do?

They led her to the top of a hill, where a man stood talking with three frogs. When Rachel stood before him he asked with disinterest, "What's your name?"

"Rachel." She knew she should not have said that.

Edmund smiled, *I will win back my sister's favor when I deliver Rachel to her!* He put on a charming smile and warmly asked, "*The* Rachel? What an honor this is! I had no idea you were in Xsardis. I am Edmund, a shape shifter. You are very welcome here. Please, won't you stay with us for a while?"

"I don't really think I have much of a choice," she retorted. "You did kidnap me."

"What? Oh yes, yes. I see what you are talking about. You think that those men were kidnapping you. No, of course not. They thought you were a threat. Shape shifters are hunted, you know. We are persecuted for no reason. And so they brought you to me to see what I had to say." Edmund was being kind for one reason: he hoped to make Rachel trust him. If he could accomplish that, she might tell him things about Xsardis that he could use to impress Sasha and Smolden, thus securing his place as leader of the shape shifters.

"For no reason? I seriously doubt that." Rachel almost laughed. "Your role has always been that of murderers and kidnappers."

"You do us a dishonor. We will let you leave if you really want," he offered.

"I do," Rachel told him, but she did not believe for a second that Edmund would let her go.

Edmund's smile turned into a grimace, "Have it your way." He called to some of the other shape shifters, "Tie her up tightly. We are going to go find Sasha."

The shape shifters moved toward Rachel. She started to run. For a moment she hoped she might be able to loose them, but it quickly became clear that without a miracle she would be captured and taken to Sasha and Smolden. *What will they do to me?* she thought. As the shape shifters caught up to her and grabbed her, Rachel let out a blood-curdling scream.

The undergrounders who had survived the earthquake numbered about seven hundred. Smolden had lost more than half his troops. The mighty beast himself was not injured from the incident but being aboveground where the gem of light could affect him had begun to make his insides churn. The pain would get worse, but what did that matter? Sasha, he trusted, would have the gem of light within the day, before its effects would kill him.

Almost every surviving undergrounder was wounded in some way. They all lay on the ground, grumbling and complaining. None of them had any interested in listening to orders or marching to Kembar Plains or fighting in Smolden's army. The dragon knew that if he did not take control of the situation quickly, most of his men would desert him. He stomped one of his massive feet to the ground for silence. The undergrounders barely noticed. Smolden let off a mighty roar, accompanied by a show of fire. The men and beasts went silent.

"We have taken great losses today," the leviathan started. The undergrounders grumbled their agreement. "But you are the ones who survived and that makes you strong. You are the elite—those whom death could not claim. Now we march on to Kembar plains and we *will* defeat the fairies. Once we have taken them down, no one will be left to stop us!

Smolden's words had the desired affect. The men held their heads up higher and began to look proud and fierce. "Stupid fairies!" one man shouted. "They're no match for us!"

"Nobody can defeat us!" another declared. Everyone began to shout out his own arrogant words as their pain turned into rage. Smolden smiled. His troops were so easily convinced.

The dragon's right hand minatour, Kerub, ordered the men, minotaurs, and toads, "Get up you lazy dogs! There is work to be done."

Seth was annoyed that he and Galen had lost sight of Rachel, but he tried not to worry. She was no wimp; Seth realized that she could hold her own.

"Look, there's a stream," Galen told Seth. "Let's take a break."

They drank from the brook and then sat down beside it. Galen could tell that Seth was troubled by not being able to see Rachel. "She's going to be alright you know. And look, the chasm is getting narrower. We should be able to cross it sometime tomorrow."

Seth was listening, but not to Galen. "Do you hear that?"

The rumble of hundreds of marching footsteps grew louder and louder.

"What in Issym?" Galen breathed. "Smolden's army. It must be."

The wanderer looked quickly about for cover. He motioned for Seth to follow him as he hid behind a huge fallen tree. As the great numbers passed by their hiding spot, Galen risked a glance upward. He saw that most of the beings were frogs but some were men. No minatours were among the ranks and the army did not walk in straight, orderly lines. Galen breathed a sigh of relief and informed Seth, "They are allies." Then he jumped to his feet and called out, "Hello there! Frogs and men, we are friends! My name is Galen and this is Seth," He pulled the teenager to his feet.

Those nearest Galen and Seth stopped and word about the two humans spread through the three hundred in their company.

A woman and a man approached them. "I am Princess Valerie and this is the captain of my army, Curt. Who are you?"

"I am Seth and this is Galen."

The princess and the captain's face lit up. The man informed them, "You are just who we are looking for. The fairy Esther told us to come find you. Your friend Rachel is in grave danger from shape shifters and we need to get to her."

"But how?" Seth asked, his face stricken with worry. He tried to trust that Rachel was tough, but if a fairy had sent an entire army to protect her, what peril did she face?

"If we can hoist one of these trees across the chasm we might be able to create a bridge."

They set to work. When it was finished Seth was the first to cross. He tried to remember all the silly cartoon movies where a scared animal or human had to cross a rickety, old bridge. When the creature in the movie looked down, he fell, but as long as he kept his head and his balance, the creature was fine.

The teen refused to look down. He moved as quickly as he dared, but the tree, though long, was not wide. As he put his first foot on land, he heard Rachel scream. Heedless of any notion of sense that would try to convince him to wait for the army of frogs and men, Seth raced toward the sound.

Sasha had been searching for hours, looking for the gem of light, but to no avail. She had done a quick search over all the clouds above Issym, torn apart the palace, looked through all the old buildings people never used, and had just finished searching through the airsprites' version of city hall.

City hall had a standard outward appearance, being made from, of course, clouds, but it was larger than any building other than the palace, and stood in the center of the airsprites' city. Inside, there were a few meeting rooms. Most of the space was taken up by one main hallway, which had pictures, artifacts, and books that told of airsprites history and legends. City hall also preserved the works of art produced by airsprites masters.

Sasha had guessed that city hall was where the gem of light would be, but she had found nothing there. She emerged from the building just in time to see birds change into human and frog forms. She was no longer the only shape shifter in the clouds. There were a few surprised faces among the airsprites at the appearance of these shifters, but no one was afraid. *Odd,* thought Sasha. *Normally people are shocked by the appearance of shifters. These creatures must often visit the airsprites.*

Jennet, the airsprite, came out and greeted one of the shape shifters, "Good to see you again, Kate!"

Kate! Sasha almost screamed. *First she robs me of Seth and now she has come here! If she gets in the way of my plans, she'll regret ever being born!*

"Hello Jennet. Is Queen Danielle around?" Kate answered.

"She is feeling ill today…but perhaps she will see you anyway."

I'm Queen Danielle! thought Sasha. *If Kate discovers who I am it could ruin everything.*

Sasha walked over to them. "How are you Kate?"

Kate bowed and smiled warmly. She looked 'Queen Danielle' in the eyes and had trouble keeping the color in her face. Sasha had learned many shape shifter abilities, but the evil woman had never learned to fully shift her eyes. They were the same every time Sasha changed form. "Good to see you," Kate managed, attempting to keep a straight face. It would be better if Sasha did not know that she had been discovered. "May we rest here for a few days?"

"Of course," Sasha answered. "I'm afraid Jennet is right, though. I am not feeling well. I should lie down."

Sasha walked towards the palace. Kate observed her go, trying to think of what to do next. Should she try to convince Jennet who the queen really was?

Jennet told them, "I'll start preparing your rooms."

Kate walked into City Hall and the other shape shifters followed her. The building was deserted so the shape shifters began to openly confer.

"What's wrong?" asked one.

"That is not Queen Danielle," Kate answered definitely.

"How can you be sure?" another questioned.

"I looked into her eyes. They say the eyes are the window to the soul, and those are not the good eyes that should belong to Queen Danielle."

"So was it Sasha?"

"Yes. Now listen up. We don't want to alert Sasha that we know who she is. We will have to lie low and try to find the gem of light before she does. Also, be on the lookout for the real Queen Danielle. Who knows where she may be hidden?" Kate worried that Sasha had killed the queen, but thought it best to keep her fears to herself. "Sasha is incredibly dangerous so wherever you go, go in groups of four or more. Okay?"

They all agreed. Kate and four others searched City Hall. They passed by pictures and statues and monuments. They came to an artist's version of the sun and the moon. The sun was made of a yellow stone and was twice as big as the moon, which was made of a white stone. They moved on, but suddenly Kate darted back and stared at the moon. The other four followed her. Kate reached out her hand and touched the work of art. Warmth and a slight tingle spread up her arm. She moved her hand away and looked at it. It was covered in some kind of paint. She glanced back at the moon. It shone brighter where she had touched it. Could it be? "The moon!" Kate announced to her friends.

"What?"

"The moon is the gem of light," she whispered.

Chapter 21

Seth was about to emerge from the woods. He could see Rachel. Her hands were tied behind her back and frogs and humans around her pushed her forward.

Seth began to wonder how he could rescue her. The frog and human army could not yet have crossed the bridge so it was him against... a lot of shape shifters. What could he do against such odds? His questions did not slow his pace.

As Seth came into Edmund's view, the shape shifter quickly realized that the teen was not one of his kind. *Who could this boy be?* Edmund asked himself as he walked over to Rachel and used his shape shifter abilities to change his hand so that it held a dagger. He put the weapon to Rachel's throat and called to Seth, "I wouldn't come any farther."

Seth stopped moving, debating what to do. Several of Edmund's men came towards him. Seth drew his sword and lunged forward, driving his blade through the stomach of the nearest man. Seth pulled the weapon out. There was not a trace of blood on it. He looked at the shifter; he had no wound.

"Drop your sword," Edmund commanded.

Seth had no choice but to comply. The shape shifters came forward and bound his hands, leading him to where Edmund held Rachel.

"You shouldn't have come!" Rachel whispered. "Now they have both of us!"

"Then you must be Seth," Edmund inferred.

The teen did not answer. He twisted his wrists, trying to break free of the rope. The cord bit into his hands, causing a burning pain.

Inwardly he chastised himself for not having stayed behind. What good was he to Rachel tied up? None. He had acted rashly and foolishly. Now Issym might pay the price.

"Tell me," the shape shifter demanded as he stared into the woods. "How many are with you?"

By now, Galen and some of the frogs and a few humans had made it across the bridge. It was slow going for only two could cross at a time. No one wanted to make a false step—there would be no surviving a fall into the deep chasm. Galen gritted his teeth as each important moment went by, anxious for Seth and Rachel's safety.

As Curt stepped down from the bridge, he noticed Galen was waiting to speak with him. "How many troops do you think we will need to fight the shifters?" the wanderer inquired.

"We probably have enough now," Curt was glad to report.

"We are blessed to have the frogs with us," Galen replied. "Without the stones in their armor, we'd never be able to stop the shape shifters."

"With any luck, they won't even fight. Shape shifters are vicious murders, but they are great cowards. They rarely fight when the stones are around and they can die."

"But Seth and Rachel would be a great prize to give to Sasha or Smolden... the shifters may well resist."

The two men quickly rounded up the part of the army that had crossed and led them through the woods, following Seth's tracks. As they entered shape shifter territory, they drew their swords and hollered their battle calls, prepared for a fight. Sensing the presence of the frog armor, the shape shifters did not resist.

Galen raced over to Seth and Rachel and untied their hands. "Are you two alright?"

"Yes, fine," Seth replied.

"It was very foolish what you did," Galen reproved. "But it is good that you both are now safe."

"Yes, good," Rachel responded.

Curt joined them, "We should leave some frogs behind to make sure these shifters don't cause any more trouble. But we need to hurry and continue on."

"Why?" Galen questioned.

"One of my scouts just reported that Smolden is aboveground. He and his army are heading north. We need to get to the fairies as soon as possible."

As Max and Arvin approached the castle, the guard at the gate inquired, "Who goes there?"

"I am here to see Princess Valerie," Arvin answered the man, who sat on a wooden stool with his feet up on a wobbly desk.

The guard stared for a second, and then his eyes flashed with recognition. "Prince Aldair!" he exclaimed, jumping to his feet and bowing.

Max looked around him for the prince. Then he saw that the guard was staring at Arvin.

"Hello Kesh," Max's companion replied.

"Where have you been? I shall alert everyone still here!"

"No. I can only stay for a little while. I'd like to speak with my sister."

"Wait…wait. *You're* Prince Aldair?" Max questioned.

"Yes. I'm sorry to deceive you, friend, but I had to make sure that you could be trusted."

Of course, Max thought. *Why would he tell me who he really is? I was working with Smolden.*

"Now Kesh, I need to see Valerie," Aldair repeated.

"She and Curt led an army of frogs and men away from here."

"What?"

"Last I heard they were heading for shape shifter territory."

Kesh quickly explained all that he knew. Prince Aldair decided, "Max and I will leave as soon as possible to join them. Please pack us some provisions and give Max a change of clothes and a sword."

"Yes sir. But... might I go with you please? It is such a dishonor to watch all the others go into battle and be left behind myself." Kesh pleaded.

Aldair thought about it, "I'm sorry. We need you here. Someone has to guard the castle."

The guard looked very disappointed but answered, "Yes, sir."

Prince Aldair and Max went into the castle. After changing, Max stood in a corridor waiting. When Arvin emerged he was a new man. Freshly shaven and wearing royal garb, Aldair looked once again like a true prince. The scars on his face were now more evident, but they added to the strength that seemed to radiate from him. He carried himself with dignity as he slipped his rapier into his belt. The man was an impressive figure. He looked liked every hero Max had ever heard of.

"So are we going to shape shifter territory?" Max asked, as they rode away from the castle. He felt grossly unworthy of keeping company with such a great man. Arvin had defied Smolden; endured his untold tortures; and then the second he got home, had left to join in a battle.

"No. The way I figure it, the only reason Smolden would go to Kembar plains is because he wants to fight the fairies. If I'm correct, than the army my sister took will head for the land of the mushnicks after they deal with the shape shifters. We'll just go straight there."

Chapter 22

Edmund and some other shifters ran through the woods, dragging Seth and Rachel with them. For this is what had happened:

After Seth had been captured, a shifter scout had informed Edmund that an army of frogs and men were crossing the chasm. Edmund made quick preparations. "You two," he ordered, "take on the shape of the prisoners. Tie yourselves up with some rope. When the frogs capture you, play the roles Seth and Rachel. You will be my spies.

"The rest of you!" he shouted, getting everyone's attention. "Don't fight the frogs. You don't stand a chance against them."

Then he chose fifteen shifters who, along with Seth and Rachel and himself, ran far from shape shifter territory. No frog or man had seen the two humans and sixteen shape shifters go, so no one came after them.

Edmund and his band of shape shifters and captives finally stopped to catch their breath. They had just sat down when stones fell from the sky and landed in their midst. Edmund jumped to his feet, aware that some kind of magic must be involved. He looked into the sky. A bird with a huge, milky-white stone in its claws was descending. When the creature landed, it turned into a woman. "Kate," Edmund's voice betrayed that he was both happy and unhappy to see her. He was glad because he always liked being around Kate, but tortured because they stood on opposite sides of a war.

The stones morphed into humans and frogs. Kate gave the gem of light to one of them. "Who are your prisoners?" she demanded, without a hint of friendliness.

Edmund sighed, "None of your business. What is that rather large object your friends are carrying?"

"None of your business," Kate mocked.

Provoked by Kate's distant attitude, Edmund grew angry. It was obvious to Seth and Rachel that this woman and Edmund were adversaries. If she was Edmund's enemy, perhaps she was their friend. "I'm Seth and this is Rachel!" Seth called out.

"Silence," Edmund hissed, pushing Seth to the ground.

"So you have managed to capture Seth and Rachel," Kate said, watching Rachel help Seth to his feet.

"And I see no reason why you would be coming down from airsprites territory carrying a large rock, unless that rock is the legendary gem of light," Edmund countered.

Kate remained silent. Edmund told her, "I can't let you leave with the gem of light in your possession."

"And I can't let you go unless you surrender Seth and Rachel," Kate responded.

"Since neither of us carry the stones of the frogs and not even Sasha knows how to kill another shape shifter without them, we are incapable of hurting each other."

"True. True. So, we are at a stand-still."

Edmund did not know if it was the right time to speak his mind, but he did anyway, "Kate, I was very saddened when you left the land of the shape shifters…"

"And I am very disappointed that you are helping your sister and Smolden take over Issym," Kate cut him off. "Don't try to remind me of your 'undying affection', Edmund. We serve two different masters."

"It's not like I *want* to aid my sister and the dragon!" Edmund retorted. "I have no doubt that Sasha and Smolden will rule cruelly. But if I don't help her… She says she can't kill another shifter, but her powers are extreme. What would you have me do?"

"We've had this battle a thousand times and you know where I stand. Fear is not a reason to do evil."

"I know."

She softened her voice in an effort to persuade him. "You think I wasn't afraid to leave? I didn't know what would happen. Like you said, your sister is dangerous and so is Smolden. But I left because I knew that Someone bigger and stronger than Sasha and the leviathan combined wanted me to help the people of Issym. God has obviously taken care of me this far; and I am confident that He will continue to do so. He would do the same for you."

Edmund shook his head, uncomfortable that the woman he loved felt like she needed to treat him like a student. "Don't lecture me," he responded.

Suddenly Sasha descended in the middle of the two groups. She first looked at Kate and declared, "I commend you for find finding the gem of light. But did you really think I'd let you keep it? Hand it over."

"No way, Sasha," Kate replied defiantly.

Sasha sighed and looked over at her brother and those with him. When her eyes landed on Seth, a leer spread across her lips. "Well, at least you haven't failed completely, Edmund. You did not subdue Kate, but you captured Seth."

"And Rachel," one of the shape shifters standing with Edmund announced.

"Marvelous," Sasha breathed. "I am going to take Seth and Rachel to Smolden at Kembar plains. You stay here and get the gem of light from Kate," she directed her brother.

"And how do you expect him to accomplish that?" Kate questioned.

Sasha eyes narrowed, "By any means necessary."

"No." Edmund barely spoke, but Sasha heard him.

"What was that?" the evil woman snapped.

Edmund's voice rose in volume and intensity, "No. I won't do it." He turned around and untied the ropes that bound Seth and Rachel's hands. "Get over to Kate. Quickly," he whispered. The two teens did as they were told and scurried across.

Sasha made no attempt to stop them. Her full attention was on her brother. "You dare to defy me!" she shouted, growing a full six inches to create a more terrifying appearance.

"Yes," Edmund answered. A smile lit up Kate's face. She wordlessly directed Seth, Rachel and two of her shifters to try to move away.

Edmund desperately tried to keep his sister's attention on himself so that she would not notice Kate and the others leaving, "I'm tired of serving you! You treat us like trash now, and it will be no different if you become queen of Issym."

"If!" Sasha was indignant. "If! Oh, I *will,* and you will rue the day you betrayed me."

"How can you be so sure that you'll defeat all of Issym? You're not a god, and the people of Issym believe they have the one true God on their side. You don't stand a chance."

Sasha laughed as if she were talking to a child and began to walk towards him, "Poor Edmund. You've listened to the lies of your beloved Kate. But I don't blame *you..." She* put her hand on his shoulder like a loving older sister would, "Just start serving me again and I won't kill you."

A shiver ran down Edmund's spine. How could she talk so calmly about killing someone! "Take your hands off me!" Edmund exclaimed, stepping away from her grip. "I won't serve you anymore. I won't help you. I may not believe everything these people believe, but I certainly agree with them that you and Smolden should never have control of Issym."

Seth, Rachel, Kate and the other good shape shifters had slipped away. Now the only ones left were Edmund, his shape shifters, and Sasha. Edmund was grateful that his shifters had not alerted Sasha of the others' disappearance. He wanted to buy Kate more time so that she get could farther away, but he did not know how long he could keep Sasha distracted. "Besides, you don't have the power to kill me." Edmund hoped that by infuriating his sister he could keep her talking.

She realized that he was taunting her and turned around to see that Kate and the others were gone. Sasha's voice exploded in a cry of rage and frustration.

She turned back toward Edmund with a deadly glare in her eyes, "You think that you have just saved the lives of Seth and Rachel and Kate, and that by doing so you have saved all Issym, don't you? Well, guess again. I will find them. And the next time our paths meet, be assured of this: no amount of begging will help you." With that, Sasha shifted into the shape of a leopard and raced off into the woods.

Edmund trembled at the thought of meeting his sister again. He looked at his band of shape shifters, "Why didn't you tell Sasha that the others were leaving?"

"We follow you, not Sasha," one answered.

"Do you still follow me? I'm joining the cause of the people of Issym."

The men and women looked at the ground. Edmund sighed, "Then you may leave."

They slowly moved away, leaving Edmund standing alone in the woods.

Smolden ordered his second in command to let the troops rest. Kerub was puzzled at this act of kindness from the dragon; but he said nothing and did as he was told.

The truth was that Smolden's pain was so fierce that he did not want to move another inch. The gem of light was steadily killing him. The agony threatened to cripple the mighty dragon. Leaving the troops behind him, Smolden sought out water with the last of his strength.

With a lake in sight, the leviathan could go no further. He lay down and clenched his teeth together, wisps of smoke coming from his nostrils. It would not be long before he was dead.

He would never have been in this position if Sasha had done her job. Nothing would give him greater pleasure than to close his jaws around her and know that she would die before he would.

Smolden thought about how his troops would mock him when they found his lifeless body. *Such a waste of my great strength,* he cursed the light.

For years he had lived in the safety of the underground, out of reach of the power of the gem of light. It had been so long he had almost forgotten what the stone could do to him. How many times had he crushed poor souls between his jaws? He had enjoyed their suffering, but was this fate now to be his own?

Unable to escape the jaws of air and earth, he longed for the water. *Water,* he hoped, his consciousness ebbing. Perhaps in it, neither the ground nor the air could reach him. Instinct and fury drove him, in one last effort, to the water's edge. He submerged his body, but no relief came. He blasted noise and fire into the air. Nothing could help him. And to think that Sasha could have prevented it, if only she had stolen the gem of light from the airsprites like she was supposed to. Why had he trusted her!

Suddenly the pain left him. One second agony was there, and the next, it was gone. He felt his strength returning. Perhaps he had not been as foolish in trusting Sasha as he had thought.

With his energy renewed, the dragon shot into the air and headed back towards his troops. Victory would be his!

He landed with a thud in front of his army and summoned Kerub. "The gem of light has been taken from the airsprites. It can harm me no longer."

"Will the shape shifter woman meet us at Kembar plains?" Kerub inquired.

"Yes," Smolden replied. "Just because I am in a good mood, make the troops move double time."

"Yes sir," answered Kerub. "Alright," hollered the minotaur. "Let's move it. You've had your break. Double time now."

Seth, Rachel, Kate, and her group of shifters were heading deeper into shape shifter territory. They had to hope that the army of frogs and men was still there.

"There are two shape shifter duplicates of us back with the frogs," Seth informed Kate as they ran.

Kate turned her head and answered, "It shouldn't be difficult to prove that you really are yourselves. All you'll have to do..." Kate crashed into something and fell to the ground.

"Sorry about that," someone said and offered her a green, three fingered hand up.

"Flibbert!" Rachel squealed with delight.

"I was looking for the two of you," the frog told Seth and Rachel.

"Well now you've found us," Seth replied, shaking his hand. "How are you?"

"Well enough. Who are your companions?"

"I am the shape shifter Kate." Flibbert almost drew his sword when she introduced herself as a shape shifter, but something about Kate's eyes made him feel that she was trustworthy. "We're on our way to join up with the army of frogs and men," she continued.

"May I join you?"

"Of course!" Rachel joyfully answered.

Sasha trailed Kate and the others until they met up with Flibbert. Then his stone armor began to affect her. She let off a growl and changed her direction. She'd have to go straight to Kembar plains without the gem of light and without Seth and Rachel.

What does it matter? she asked herself. *The gem is not in the clouds—it can't hurt Smolden. I'll just tell him that I've hidden it. And the dragon never needs to know that I ran into Seth and Rachel.*

A smug smile spread across her face, *Even with all the victories that the people of Issym have won, they will be no match for the undergrounder army, Smolden and myself!*

Chapter 23

The army of frogs and humans was marching out of shape shifter's territory. They were forced to leave forty-five of their men behind to keep the shifters in check. Galen, Seth and Rachel were about to join the army's walk, but Galen sensed something wrong with the two teens. He could not put his finger on it, but he knew something just was not right.

He looked them over. Seth appeared the same but Rachel seemed to be missing something. "Rachel! The necklace—where is it?"

"What necklace?" asked the fake Rachel.

"The necklace Orvan gave you."

"Orvan?" she started. "Oh, right, Orvan," she added, trying to play the part. "I lost it."

"And you're alright?"

"Of course I am. Why shouldn't I be?"

"The acena virus..."

No recognition dawned in the shape shifter's eyes. "Why," concluded Galen, "you're not Rachel at all."

"What are talking about? Of course she's Rachel," Seth put in.

"Is she? What's my name?" Galen asked.

"Um... Stephen?" Rachel guessed.

"No."

"Rachel! What's wrong with you?" The counterfeit Seth had to turn on the other shape shifter or else his own cover would be blown.

"Seth, do you know what my name is?" Galen inquired.

"Of course I do... why would you ask such a silly question?"
"I just need to be sure. What's my name?"
"Paseah?"
Galen had a pretty good guess what was going on. He called for Curt, who was in charge of the army for the time being.
"Well?" Curt asked shortly.
"I think we have a phony Seth and Rachel."
"Why?"
"They didn't know my name."
At that moment, the real Seth and Rachel, along with Flibbert and the good shape shifters, emerged from the trees. Curt saw them. He told Galen as he pointed in their direction, "I think you're right."

Seth and Rachel picked up their speed when they saw Galen. In the time they had been in Issym they had met lots of nice people, but Galen was their closet ally. They desperately wanted just to be back beside him, knowing beyond doubt that he would give his life to protect theirs. "Those are impostors!" Seth and Rachel shouted in unison.

"What's my name?" Galen asked, wanting to be sure that these were not new impostors.

"Galen, of course," Rachel replied, now standing beside him.

"Good to see that you are alright," Galen smiled. Curt ordered that the phony Seth and Rachel be taken away.

"Galen, I would like you to meet Flibbert," Seth introduced proudly.

"Nice to meet you," Flibbert responded without enthusiasm, remembering Esther the fairy's words of caution.

"And you as well. I've heard much about you," the man replied, his voice far more cheerful than the frog's.

Meanwhile, Curt spoke with Kate. "Were you able to stop Sasha?"

"Not exactly. We brought the gem of light with us," she answered.

"But now Smolden is free to roam the land as he wishes!"

"She was pretending to be the airsprites' queen. We couldn't just leave it there for Sasha to find! "

"I understand that, I guess. But us having the gem is almost as bad as Smolden having it—almost."

"I'm sorry. I just..."

"It's all right. You made the best decision you could."

"With your permission I would like to go back to the enchanted clouds for a little while. There are some things I need to do. For starters, I'd like to find Queen Danielle—Sasha must have hidden her somewhere in order to take her place."

"All right. Meet us as soon as you can at the land of the mushnicks."

"My people will go with you and carry the gem of light. I will meet you there."

Kate set off and the shape shifters, Seth, Rachel, Galen, Flibbert, and Curt joined in the march of the army. Rachel walked beside Princess Valerie and the two spent the entire day talking. When evening came the princess picked some of her own clothes and gave them to Rachel, whose attire was all muddy and torn from days of walking and the earthquake she had barely managed to survive. The teen put them in her pack and settled down to sleep.

Edmund started to walk toward his home. He intended to meet up with the army and join them in their march to the land of the fairies and mushnicks. He slowly ambled along, letting his thoughts take reign, until he saw someone walking towards him. It was Kate.

"Edmund I've been looking for you," Kate told him.

He smiled. Kate had come looking for *him.* "Why? Is everything alright?"

"Sasha kidnapped Queen Danielle and I think you're the only person who can tell me where the airsprites queen is. She needs to be freed."

"Why do you think I can help?"

"Because you're as close to your sister as a person can get."

Edmund grimaced, "Sasha has several underground hideaways and I'm betting she put Danielle in one of them."

"Do you know where they are?"

"Follow me."

Chapter 24

Edmund and Kate morphed into jaguars and ran for several miles. When they stopped, Kate and Edmund turned back into human form.

"Well, where is Sasha's hideout?" Kate questioned.

Edmund pushed away some of the debris that had been caused by the earthquake. This revealed a thin, but wide gray stone, which Edmund pulled away to expose a medium sized hole in the ground. Edmund expected to hop into the opening and help Kate down, but rubble from the earthquake had created a staircase. He and Kate descended into the tunnel.

It was too dark to see anything in the hollow ground, so Kate and Edmund each shifted their right hands so that they were holding torches. Thanks to the light they saw that they were standing in a small tunnel—only wide enough to walk single file—and that not far from the entrance, the tunnel took a sharp curve to the left. "Have you been here before?" Kate whispered. She could not explain why she felt the need to speak softly, but there was something eerie about the tunnel.

"Once," Edmund replied. "If we take that turn we will come into Sasha's storage room. If Danielle is in this tunnel, that is where she'll be."

"Is this a part of Smolden's underground?"

"No, the underground lies much deeper in the earth."

The two shifters walked a few paces to the curve and went around the bend. Suddenly they saw a dwarf with an ax running straight at them. Edmund had no time to dodge as the dwarf threw his blade into Edmund's chest. The dwarf smiled, but the shape shifter simply pulled the weapon from his body. Then he reached out and picked the little man up by his beard. "That's not very nice," Edmund stated. "Kate, will you get some rope so that we may tie up our little friend here."

They bound their assailant and set him down on the ground. He was a common dwarf with a long beard and a head that came up to their waists, but there was something uncommon about his being in the tunnel. "Don't dwarves live in Asandra?" Kate asked, "and *only* in Asandra?"

"No dwarf has ever set foot on Issym before," Edmund agreed, "or at least that I know of." They looked around the room; it was not very large but it contained nearly fifteen barrels with room for more. Kate's eyes landed on Queen Danielle. Her hands were bound, her mouth was gagged and she seemed to be in a deep sleep.

"Tell us dwarf, why are you on Issym?" Edmund commanded with an air of authority.

"Whatever *she* wishes *she* gets," the dwarf hissed.

"How many others did Sasha bring from Asandra?" Edmund questioned.

The dwarf was silent. "How many?" he bellowed.

"Not many. Queen Sasha has lots of servants on Asandra, but much fewer here."

"My sister is not a queen."

"Her majesty *is* a queen," the dwarf insisted passionately. "You weaklings may not know it yet, but she *will* be queen of all Xsardis. No one can stop her."

Kate pulled Edmund aside and whispered too quietly for their prisoner to hear, "If that dwarf spoke truthfully and there are others around working for Sasha, we could be in danger. We should get Queen Danielle out of here and go back to the airsprites."

"That dwarf could know more about Sasha's plans," Edmund fought back.

"It's too risky."

"We're not important to Issym's victory so it's okay to take risks. We've played our part by getting the gem of light and Seth and Rachel to the army. Now, we have a chance to find out about my sister's plans and I'm taking it."

"Fine—stay here, but I'm going to wake up Danielle and get out of here. Whether or not you come is up to you."

"How do you intend to arouse the queen?"

"Long ago the shape shifters had great powers and the knowledge of herbs and roots. Now we have lost most of them, but your sister has studied deeply into our past and rediscovered many of them. I have as well. You'd be surprised by what I can do."

Kate took a vial from the folds of her dress and poured a little of the concoction into Danielle's mouth. Within seconds the queen's eyes were open.

Kate untied the airsprite's mouth and hands. "Thank goodness you're here, Kate," Danielle exclaimed.

"We've got to get out of here, quickly," the shape shifter replied.

The queen was too weak to walk on her own, but with Kate and Edmund's help she gained her footing and walked out of the tunnel. Once outside Kate spoke, "Are you coming with us to the enchanted clouds, Edmund?"

Edmund took a breath. A huge part of him wanted to go wherever Kate was and to win her heart and have her as his wife, but the other part of him knew that Kate was dedicated to her mission and her God. Unless Edmund became a Christian he was sure that Kate would not have him as her husband. And he was not going to start believing in some imaginary creature any time soon.

Edmund realized that he could not help the people of Issym by going with Kate and Queen Danielle. If he tried to join the frog army, he would not be trusted. Edmund began to feel as if he had no place in the world. Perhaps the best course of action would be to stay and find out what the dwarf knew. He was sure that this creature was not the only one of Sasha's servants around and Kate was right, it was risky to stay; but he was the right person to take a risk. He was of no value to anyone, he thought. If by risking his life he could serve the people of

Issym, he would remain and question the dwarf further. "I'm going to stay."

"Okay," she answered, her voice unsure. She did not know why her lips trembled. Surely she had put Edmund and their love behind her!

Edmund, with determination on his face, turned and reentered the tunnel.

Danielle was regaining her strength. In a matter of minutes she would be able to fly to the clouds of the airsprites. "After Sasha kidnapped you, she took your place," Kate filled her in. "She was trying to steal the gem of light. The only way to protect the gem was to take it and give it to the people of Issym,"

"Kate, how could you?"

"What else could we do? We could not risk the gem falling into Sasha's hands. What if she had destroyed it? Or given it to Smolden?"

Danielle nodded, clearly troubled.

"I fear your people will think that we kidnapped you and stole the gem of light."

"You did steal the gem," replied the young queen, "but I will convince them of your intentions."

Danielle and Kate flew up to the clouds. When they arrived, the airsprites tried to arrest Kate; but Danielle calmed them and explained everything to them. With quiet determination, she spoke to her people of the love Issym's creatures had shown them throughout the ages, and of their duty to help them in return. Many agreed, and with their queen, set out for the land of the mushnicks and fairies.

Halfway through the night, Seth woke as someone shook his shoulder. He opened his eyes and made out from the darkness the shape of a frog. The creature held a finger to his lips for silence and motioned that Seth should follow.

The frog led Seth past the sleeping army members and towards the woods. As Seth started to wake up, he realized that it was foolish to follow an unknown figure away from the group. When they walked past a torch the teen watched carefully to see if he could figure out who was leading him. It was Flibbert. Seth's mind and heart were at ease. Flibbert was trustworthy.

As they came near the woods Seth saw that another figure was already waiting for them. It was Rachel. "Quickly, into the woods," Flibbert commanded.

"What are you talking about, Flibbert?" Rachel inquired.

"It's not safe. The fairy Esther told me to take you two away from the group. Who knows if all the frogs and humans here are really trustworthy? What if they kidnapped you and took you to Smolden? Then our only hope for Issym would be destroyed!"

"Who would kidnap us? That's silly!" Rachel told him.

"I'm going back to sleep," Seth added. "Trekking through the woods in the middle of the night, away from the army, doesn't sound like fun. Besides, everybody will be worried about us and think that you kidnapped us."

"I left a note," Flibbert answered. "Now, come on. We really do have to go. What the fairy said makes sense."

"Maybe," Rachel replied, "it makes sense to you, but not to me."

Flibbert grunted. This was a lot harder than he had thought. "Come on you two, don't you trust me? I'm doing this for your own good."

"But how does going *away* from the army help keep us safe?" Seth questioned. "Flibbert, you normally make more sense."

"Think about how much of a reward Smolden would give for the delivery of either of you," Flibbert told them. "Now, think about Max. He, your friend, would turn you in for that kind of money."

The mention of Max made Seth's stomach turn. What had happened to him? "He's right," Seth gave in.

"Fine," Rachel conceded.

Flibbert had packed a bag full of provisions. Rachel and Seth both carried their packs. Rachel had her dagger strapped around her waist and Seth and Flibbert both had their swords. With these few items the trio headed into the woods.

One of the frog sentries that had been posted saw them talking, but while he was looking away they slipped into the forest. The sentry assumed they had gone back to bed and so Seth, Flibbert and Rachel escaped into the woods without being noticed.

When daylight came, the three found a deep pool of water. They stopped at its banks and had breakfast. No one said much. They were exhausted from walking through the night.

After breakfast, Seth and Flibbert went further into the woods to change and Rachel went in the opposite direction. As she pulled on her boots, she called out to let them know she was ready. There was no response.

She walked forward, trying to decide whether or not Princess Valerie would mind if she tore the sleeves off her dress. Valerie had been kind to lend her the garment, but it was long and had flowing sleeves. It did not lend itself to woods walking. She ripped the bottom and the arms off the dress and stuffed the fabric in her bag.

"Hello!" she called again. No answer. "Guys!" she tried to make her voice louder.

She came to a clearing. There were no trees or bushes, only stones. Beyond the rocks, tall, mature trees grew on either side of a path of rich brown dirt.

Rachel made her way to the line of trees. The moment she stepped onto the path, she saw Flibbert and Seth lying on the road. "Wake up, guys! No time to sleep," she called out teasingly. They did not respond. "Flibbert. Seth. Get up! Hello?"

If they were taking a nap, they certainly could not be comfortable. Seth's body was twisted in a strange manor. Flibbert was lying face down. *What's going on?* she wondered, becoming scared. *Maybe some of the undergrounders found them, knocked them unconscious—or worse—and are now waiting to trap me as well.*

Rachel's senses were on high alert. She held her breath, listening for any sound of assailants. She heard nothing.

As the teen closed the distance between herself and her companions, she picked up speed. To her surprise no one came forward to seize her as she dropped to the ground beside her unconscious allies. She rolled Flibbert over. He did not have the normal, healthy green tint to his skin, but Rachel was no expert in frog anatomy.

She put Seth's head in her lap. He was alive but his breathing was shallow and his face was pale. *What happened?* she asked herself.

She spoke his name, softly at first, and then louder: "Seth. Seth!" He did not stir.

She watched as he became deathly pale—a grayish color—and his shallow breaths became farther and farther apart. Rachel's eyes started to water and she put her hand on his forehead, which was moist with a deep sleep. She could find no wound on Seth or Flibbert, so what could have caused this? *What do I do, God?* she prayed, as her fallen companions seemed to grow worse.

Chapter 25

As Rachel held Seth's head she looked up. Through her tears she saw a great many lights coming towards her. At first they looked like unconnected Christmas tree lights. As they got closer she saw that the tiny spheres, smaller than her hand, seemed to be alive. They appeared to consist only of light and came in multitudes of different colors. As they moved, occasionally small light sparks would fall from them to the ground.

As they got closer, Rachel began to feel tired. *How can I be sleepy at a time like this?* she asked herself. Yet her head began to fall forward and it was with great difficultly that she kept her eyelids open. *This must be why Seth and Flibbert fell asleep.* It was the only logical conclusion.

Rachel was a strong-willed person and determined not to let the creatures succeed in making her fall asleep; but she knew that she could only resist for so long. Soon she would give in to the slumber calling her name. A buzzing noise came from one of the creatures. *I know that sound!* Rachel thought.

More buzzing followed. *If only I could remember!* Rachel racked her brain. It sounded like they were talking to each other.

One red creature came over to her and seemed to be looking at her (though why she thought that was a mystery to Rachel, for the creature had no eyes, nor any other features). It gave off two short buzzes.

Rachel felt the sleepiness receding and tried hard to think. Memories pounded at her brain's door desperately trying to come out but something stopped them. The creature moved back and Rachel felt exhaustion sweep over her again. *Think, Rachel, think!*

The teen imitated the creatures' buzzes with a slight variation. She was pretty sure that she had said something but was not sure what. The creature came forward once again. It gave off a series of buzzes and Rachel tried to interpret it. The first buzz could be a 'do' and the third a 'speak' and the fourth an 'our' but the other two words she could not make out. Perhaps they had asked, "Do you speak our language?"

"I do," Rachel hoped she buzzed. The tiredness left.

"Who are you?"

"I am Rachel."

"Do you know who we are?"

"I only faintly recall you," she tried to say.

Another creature, this time colored blue, moved forward and told her, "We are the illuminescents. You created us. One of us remembered you."

"Why do you want to hurt my friends?"

"These are your friends?"

"Yes."

Rachel heard Seth take a deeper breath and then a deeper one. His color started to return. Finally he opened his eyes. She asked the illuminescents, "And the frog? Will you heal him too?"

"We would, but how do we know he won't hurt us?"

"You attacked us—not the other way around."

"The frogs steal us from the air with their tongues," the red one answered. In her mind, Rachel named her Ruby.

"What's going on?" Seth asked, sitting up, trying to understand the humming coming from the flying lights.

"The creatures made of light are the illuminescents," Rachel informed him. "The buzzing is their language."

Oh that explains everything! Seth thought sarcastically.

The illuminescents withdrew and conversed among themselves. Rachel thought she could hear the little red one loudly insisting, against all the others' better judgment, that they should wake Flibbert. The illuminescents came back towards the three companions. "We will wake the frog." Apparently the little one had persuaded them. They moved backward as Flibbert sat up.

"I was sure I was a goner there. I had heard about a forest that puts everyone to sleep. A tale is told to our younglings of a wood where slumber can cause death. Those who flee have a chance at life, but those who linger are never seen again. I never thought I would happen across it!" Flibbert's voice was jolly, but there was a tremble in it, as if he only pretended to be brave. This place seemed to have taken him back to his childhood around the campfire, where the line between reality and make-believe had blurred; where teenage frogs tell stories to disturb the young ones' sleep, and you are never sure if things are said to scare you or to warn you. "We need to get out of here," he added, lowering his voice. He adjusted his stance so that he could spring at a moment's notice.

"You mean you think that these creatures have actually killed?" Rachel questioned, taking a sharp breath. It was painful to think of her beloved creatures doing this. When alone as a young child, they were her imaginary playmates. When sad, they comforted her. When sleepless, they helped her to rest. And now they had turned that peaceful sleep into...

"Yes, many," Flibbert responded, interrupting her thoughts.

"Why have you killed so many?" Rachel asked the illuminescents incredulously.

"Killed?" inquired the red one.

"Yes, killed, like you would have my companions and I."

"We have not killed them," a green one replied. "Just put them to sleep. A long time ago we lived on Asandra. We had a friendly life and were peaceful creatures.

"But then, we were attacked and almost all of us were killed. We did not know how to defend ourselves. Only five of us remained alive and those five fled here.

"We hid in this forest and learned how to defend ourselves. We tried to warn the first intruders not to come into our forest but they attacked us, killing another of our number. Other creatures followed," they continued, keeping their distance from Flibbert. "We couldn't risk being attacked again so we now put everyone who comes here to sleep."

"Just to sleep?" Rachel questioned. "So they can be awakened?"

"Yes," Ruby replied, with more energy in her one word than the green illuminescent had put in his entire tale.

Flibbert, impatient to leave, spoke to Rachel, "We should get out of here while we still can." For once in his life, the frog wanted to flee. The stories had heard about this forest when he was a child haunted him, and it disturbed him not to be able to understand the conversation.

Rachel was inclined to trust these creatures. She ignored the frog and hummed, "Why did you try to talk to me?"

"I was only a child when the attack against my people happened on Asandra," Ruby told her. "My parents brought me here but I became ill, so they put me to sleep until they could learn how to wake me up. My people recently found a cure for my disease and aroused me. I remembered you, because I was one of the first you created and therefore, I had seen you."

Rachel was not sure she understood, but there were more important things to discuss, "Where are those you put to sleep?"

"We will show you. Follow us."

Rachel told Seth and Flibbert, "I'll explain everything but right now we need to follow the illuminescents."

"Are you sure they can be trusted?" Seth questioned.

"As sure as I can be. They seem good."

"No thank you," Flibbert declared. "I'm going back out of the forest and finding another way to the mushnicks."

"They say that everyone who has ever come here has not been killed but put to sleep. They can be woken up!" Rachel exclaimed. "The illuminescents are going to take us to them."

"So let me get this straight," Flibbert started. "You want me to follow you through the woods led by strange, glowing, buzzing creatures that put us to sleep so that they can take us to where the rest of their prisoners are? No way!"

"Please Flibbert," Seth urged. He had confidence in Rachel's judgment, although his own gut told him not to trust the illuminescents.

"Fine," Flibbert conceded sourly. His feet would move but his distrust would not.

Galen rushed over to Princess Valerie and Curt, "Seth and Rachel are gone."

"Don't be hasty," Curt replied. "There are hundreds of frogs, humans, and shape shifters here. They must be around somewhere. Where would they go?"

"You said it yourself, there are hundreds of people here. And can you vouch for the character of them all? The rewards Smolden would offer if Seth and Rachel were delivered to him would be very great."

"You're overreacting," Princess Valerie told Galen, "but all the same I will instruct some troops to look for them." Frogs and men started searching.

Meanwhile, a frog came up to Galen, the princess and Curt. He cleared his throat to get their attention. "Pardon me, but last night I saw Flibbert and Seth and Rachel standing beside the woods. When I looked again they were gone. I assumed they went back to sleep."

"What?" cried Galen. "You only tell us this now!"

The man lowered his head. "I had no reason to think anything of it. Why would they leave?"

A man stepped next to Curt, "I just found this letter."

Galen grabbed the letter and read it aloud:

I, Flibbert the frog, have escorted Seth and Rachel into the woods for their own protection. The fairy Esther told me that I should take them away, in order to keep them safe. In a group so large, we could not ensure their security. Don't worry; we'll meet you in the land of the fairies and mushnicks.

For Issym's victory,
Flibbert

Valerie took the letter, "My brother and I have received many letters from Flibbert so I know his hand."

"Did he write it?" Galen asked.

"Yes."

"How trustworthy is he?"

"Very."

Chapter 26

Rachel, Flibbert, and Seth followed the illuminescents through the woods. In a little under half a mile they reached their destination—a clearing where about fifty creatures lay in a deep, magical sleep. Rachel stepped in, but Flibbert stopped Seth just outside. From where the frog was standing, he could reach Rachel in a single leap or strike the illuminescents with his tongue.

The sleeping frogs and humans were all gray. Unless she had looked at them intently Rachel would have thought they were dead or statues. Upon a closer examination of one frog beside her, however, she saw that he took a shallow breath from time to time.

"Can you wake them up?" Rachel buzzed in the illuminescent language.

"We are capable," Ruby replied.

"Will you?" Rachel rephrased.

Another illuminescent spoke up, "What guarantee do we have that they will not attack us?"

Flibbert called to Rachel (since neither he nor Seth spoke the illuminescent language), "What's going on?"

"I'm trying to convince them to wake everyone," Rachel answered. "They want to know how they can be sure that no one will hurt them."

"They can't be sure!" Flibbert mocked. "They are evil creatures!"

"Flibbert, stop being so afraid and get in here. It was all a misunderstanding. If they had wanted to harm us, they would have done it before now. Why do you think that they put everyone to sleep and didn't kill them?"

"If they were really good and it was all a misunderstanding, why don't they wake them up now?"

"I told you, they are scared."

Rachel went back to talking with Ruby. "How exactly do you wake people up? Does every one of you have to be involved or just one?"

"I can wake them up one at a time by myself," Ruby replied.

"Can you convince two others to help you? Because if you could, the rest of your people could retreat to the trees and just you three stay. When you wake someone up, either I or one of my companions would be there to make sure they do not hurt you."

Ruby went away and talked with her people. Rachel filled Seth and Flibbert in on her plan and everything she remembered and had learned about the illuminescents.

Ruby came over with a blue and a green illuminescent, "Two have agreed."

They began the task of waking up the captives. "Where am I?" the frog or human would ask.

"You are safe. We'll explain everything in a short amount of time. Just be careful; don't attack any of the little, glowing, round creatures who come near you," was the reply.

When everyone was awake, Rachel shouted for silence. She was not loud enough so Flibbert hollered for her. When they were quiet, Rachel addressed them, "Hello everyone! I know you must have a lot of questions but please, listen to what I have to say.

"My name is Rachel and this is Seth—we are the ones who imagined Xsardis. With us is Flibbert, the guard of the airsprites' gate. In case you were wondering, the little creatures hovering around you are the illuminescents. They put you to sleep to defend themselves, but it was a mistake. That is why they have now awoken you.

"I'm not sure how long some of you have been asleep or what has happened in Issym since then, but this I can tell you: the evil dragon Smolden and his troops are moving towards Kembar plains. Their plan is to attack the fairies and then conquer the rest of Issym. They must be stopped at all costs.

"Many other frogs and humans are on their way to the country of the mushnicks and fairies as we speak. They will try to keep them safe. But we need your help too."

Flibbert picked up where Rachel left off, "I know you all would like to return to your homes and find out what happened to your families since you fell asleep, but I ask you to help Issym. We need all the fighting troops we can get. By protecting the fairies, you will be protecting yourselves and your families from great evil. Any of you willing, follow me now!"

Flibbert started to leave the woods and some followed, but many seemed hesitant. Rachel could understand why; if she had been asleep for years, her first priority would be to find what was left of her family. Ruby came to her, "We want to help too."

As they joined the others in heading down the path, Rachel asked Ruby, "So what is your name?"

"I don't have one. Illuminescents do not call each other by names," she responded.

"Oh."

"You could give me one, though," she offered.

"Okay. How about Ruby?"

"I like it."

They walked on. Seth found it interesting to listen to the conversations around him. He had been walking with Rachel at first, but she would not stop talking to Ruby. The buzzing language of the illuminescents gave him a headache. Seth had moved away and started listening to the others. They were from various periods of history and it was intriguing to hear their accents, their stories, and their views on life.

With Flibbert leading the group, Rachel talking to illuminescents, and Seth conversing with the re-awakened frogs and men, the days of their journey to the land of the mushnicks and fairies passed quickly.

The frogs, humans, and shape shifters, led by Curt, Princess Valerie, and Galen, reached the land of the mushnicks only a few hours before Seth, Rachel and the others did. Lady Amber, who had gathered troops from the other half of the continent, had arrived with many additional soldiers.

As Seth and Rachel first entered this area, they only saw bright, colorful stone houses. As they went further in, they noticed greater numbers of plain, wooden dwellings. Rachel surmised that the vibrant houses belonged to the mushnicks and the boring ones to the fairies. Tents were set up on every available space. Mushnicks bustled about taking care of the guests who had already arrived. The clanging of multiple smithies and the racket of sword clashing against sword, as men and frogs practiced, made an overwhelming din.

The mushnicks were just as Rachel had envisioned them. They were happy, plump, short and colorful. She was disappointed, however, to find that the fairies were nowhere to be seen.

When Galen saw Seth and Rachel he immediately moved towards them. "Next time, let me come along. You had us all worried."

Before they could reply, a mushnick carrying a basket bigger than he was ran right into Rachel and dropped it. "Sorry," he apologized, hurriedly picking up the apples that had fallen out.

"What's your name?" Rachel asked as she bent down to help him.

"Troy. And who are you?"

"I'm Rachel."

The mushnick dropped the apples he had gathered. Grabbing her hand, he exclaimed, "Then I must take you to see the fairies! They're having a *big* meeting. Where is Seth?"

"Right here," Seth answered.

"Come along then," Troy said, pulling them forward. "Time to meet the fairies."

Galen would have followed the two teenagers, but he was distracted by a conversation going on between Flibbert and a frog woman.

"You gathered a lot of people for the battle, Amber. You have my thanks," Flibbert was saying.

"The frogs and humans on the north side of Issym are very valiant," Amber replied. "Those near Smolden's mountain have suffered greatly as of late. The villains from Mt. Smolden are attacking the nearby villages. If they don't steal cattle or food, they burn the crop fields for pleasure. Most of the frogs and humans living there are worried that they won't have enough food to make it through the winter. But even in these conditions they have joined in the battle."

"If we win the war against Smolden it will give them some relief, won't it?"

"I don't think so. The criminals live on Mt. Smolden, but not all of them work for the vile beast. Whether Smolden lives or Smolden dies make no difference to most of the thieves."

"Don't the villagers fight back?"

"They do, but they fight by themselves. When the men from the mountain try to steal from one village, that town, and that town only, battles against them. At first, this held off the attackers, but now, the criminals come in larger numbers and the individual towns cannot fight them off. Many good men and frogs have been wounded or even killed."

Galen jumped into the conversation, "They have to fight together. Someone should lead them in an attack that does more than defend their crops and livestock against a few thieves. They need to get on the offensive and purge the mountain of the villains. Then, and only then, will they be free from the scoundrels and be safe in their own homes!"

Galen then added, "Please excuse me. Your conversation interested me. I'm Galen."

"Amber," she replied as she heard Curt call out to Galen. The wanderer excused himself and left.

"He's right," Amber told Flibbert. "They do need someone to join them together and lead an offensive attack."

"And Galen's just the one to do it," agreed Flibbert.

Chapter 27

Edmund descended back into the tunnel. As he rounded the bend he saw the dwarf biting at the ropes that held him. "So," Edmund began, "my sister's a queen, eh?"

"Yes."

"Is she queen of Asandra?"

"Not yet, but she will be. She has an army and they work day and night to prepare weapons. They train and gather new recruits. The only reason she is not queen yet is because she desires eternal youth. Once she acquires that, she will return to Asandra and win the continent. Then she will kill Smolden and be ruler of all Xsardis."

The dwarf was speaking freely of Sasha's goals. He probably did not even realize that while he bragged about his master, he was helping Edmund learn her plans.

"How does she intend to kill Smolden?"

"She will find a way."

"How many of Sasha's servants are on Issym?"

"Only me," the dwarf replied. "There were five of us, but the others were not competent enough for the queen."

How could Sasha kill people without even thinking? That was why Edmund had to stop her. He realized that more than just Issym was on the line. All of Xsardis was in danger. Even if she lost the battle in Issym, if she gained eternal youth she would think it a victory.

One more sword would not help Issym in the battle, but perhaps he could help Xsardis by spying out Sasha's army in Asandra.

As Seth and Rachel followed Troy the mushnick, they asked where they were going. He answered, "The fairies are waiting for you in the main building."

Three stories high and shaped like a circle, the main building contrasted the simplicity of the fairy houses. The outside had been built with a shimmering bark, which reminded Seth and Rachel of the grove of trees in Valinor. Its windows and doors had been carefully shaped from branches of the same kind of tree. The staircase that wrapped around the building looked sturdy and beautiful. The steps had been formed from what appeared to be blue leaves, which Rachel bent over to touch. They were soft and yet steady. "Could this be from the Valinor trees we saw?" she asked Seth.

"Yes," Troy told them. "The fairies send us every year to take one tree, but they always grow back. We let nothing of the precious tree go to waste."

As Troy, Rachel, and Seth entered, they saw that the entire building was one huge room. Each level but the first had a hole in the middle, and nothing but seating on what floor there was. The ground was made of the same leaves that had formed the outside steps. The ceiling seemed to be a clear roof, which let in the sunlight.

All eyes were on Seth and Rachel as they meekly stepped into the center of the first floor. Countless fairies filled almost every seat. Troy withdrew. The teens were sad to see him go, since that left them as the only non-fairies in the building.

"Um…Hello," started Seth, feeling like a hole was being bored into his head by the fairies' staring. "I am Seth and this is Rachel. You sent for us."

"We did," answered a female fairy on the first floor. She was a fairy of the blue and wore a slender crown. Her dress was ornate and her eyes and wings were covered in blue spirals.

The male fairy of the green beside her, presumably the king based on the crown sitting on his head, walked into the center of the building so that everyone could see him. Then he spoke, "My fellow fairies, we all know the circumstances that have brought us here. I need not remind anyone of the cruelty of Smolden and his fellow conspirator Sasha the shape shifter; nor do I need to inform you that we have an army of valiant creatures from all over Issym willing to fight with us. I am sure you all are aware of these things and the honor we have to see Seth and Rachel, imaginers of Xsardis, here with us." The king turned to Seth and Rachel. "You will help us?"

They nodded.

"Then let us begin our preparations to defeat the dragon and his minions."

Every fairy in the building rose and bowed their heads. *What are they doing?* Seth wondered at first, but then the king began to pray and Seth understood. The teen thought it was very fitting that they should ask God's guidance before they made their plans on how to fight against the undergrounders. He silently offered up his own prayer, *I don't know what I'm doing, but I want to help these people. Please, give us guidance and strength.*

An hour later, Seth and Rachel were still in the main building, but much had changed. Most of the fairies had left and some humans and frogs had arrived. There were about twenty-five people sitting around a large table that had been set up in center of the first floor. Each fairy, frog and human was there for a specific reason. Some, like Curt, were military leaders. Others, like the king and queen of the fairies, were very important royalty. Still others, like Seth and Rachel were simply special. Galen the fort ruler, Ruby the illuminescent, and Flibbert the frog were also present.

The king of the fairies introduced Elimelech, the fairy army captain. Elimelech, who was a fairy of the green, got right to the point. "We have three major things to focus on in this battle," he declared. "The first is Smolden's army. Our scouts report that it is large, but so is ours.

"The second is Sasha the shape shifter. She is very powerful and can be in many, I've heard hundreds, of different forms at once. As you know shape shifters cannot be killed, unless the stones the frogs carry are present. There are plenty of frogs going out to battle and each one has stone armor; therefore, Sasha can be killed, but she still will greatly add to Smolden's army. As a result, he will almost certainly outnumber us.

"The third and worst problem is the dragon himself. He cannot be injured; we have found no weakness in him. The gem of light would ordinarily prevent him from being above ground, but in order to prevent it from falling into Smolden's hands, we have had to bring the gem here and…"

"I have an idea," someone interrupted. It was Seth who had spoken. Every eye was on him.

"What is it?" asked the king of the fairies.

Seth could not believe he was speaking to a war council; he almost stopped. Who was he to give suggestions to the wisest people in all of Issym? He took a breath and continued, "I'm not sure this will work, but it's worth a try. We know that the gem of light can kill Smolden if it is in the right place and that no weapon ever crafted has been able to damage the dragon. But what if we formed the gem of light into a sword? It certainly has powers over Smolden. If we gave the weapon to the best fighter and had him attack Smolden with it, perhaps he could succeed in killing the beast."

Everyone agreed. It was a logical plan. Galen and Rachel were surprised. They both remembered the Seth who did not want to fight in the battle in the first place; now he was coming up with good strategies.

"Very good," Elimelech declared. "Now what about Sasha? Is there anything that can be done to stop her from multiplying herself?"

In that room were the best and brightest fairies, humans and frogs in Issym, but no one had any suggestions.

Ruby the illuminescent buzzed to Rachel, "Tell them what I told you."

"Not right now," Rachel answered. "We're not talking about Smolden."

Ruby waited a few more seconds and tried again, "Tell them."

"No!" Rachel replied. Seth might have been brave enough to address the war council, but she was certainly not.

"You need to tell them," the illuminescent insisted in a tone that sounded like the high pitched buzzing that comes from some electronics on earth and gives people headaches.

"Alright," Rachel finally agreed.

Rachel cleared her throat, "Excuse me, my little friend here has a message she wants me to give you.

"She is an illuminescent. Many of her people are here and they want to help us. They say that they have certain powers that might be of assistance. Those of her kind that are green, for example, can increase speed. The blue ones, like blue fairies, can heal. The yellow ones can make a person fly.

"They have increased powers if they all work together. Ruby says that is possible to make it so Smolden could not breathe fire for about two hours. The illuminescents would then be completely drained of ability for some time."

"Happy now?" she buzzed to Ruby.

"Yes," the little illuminescent replied.

"Give her our thanks," the fairy king responded. "We would welcome their help."

After this, the meeting seemed to go on forever. They talked and discussed and debated whether they should attack Smolden or defend themselves, when they should do this and how it should be done. Seth added a few things every now and again and Rachel spoke once more, but for the most part decisions were left to people like Curt and Elimelech, who understood battles. When they finally retired for the evening, it was late and everyone was worn out.

Seth and Rachel walked out of the building without saying much to each other. They moved to one of the many fires lit throughout the camp. Troy the mushnick brought them plates of dinner. Neither spoke but both inwardly thought, *How on Xsardis are we to win this battle? I don't know what I'm doing!*

The two teens listened to the noise of the land. Every inch was covered with frogs, mushnicks, fairies, humans and illuminescents. Some were polishing armor; some were sharpening swords; some were talking; some were laughing. Seth heard a familiar laugh. *It can't be,* he thought. It sounded like Max.

Seth looked around to find the source of the sound. He saw his friend's face. "Max!" shouted Seth, jumping to his feet.

The teen heard someone call his name and saw Seth and Rachel coming towards him. He walked away from Princess Valerie and Prince Aldair without even a polite, "Excuse me."

Max stood beside them. "I've got a lot to say and you better just let me spit it out," he started. Then he described to Seth and Rachel everything that had happened. He concluded with, "I've learned so much and I'm really sorry for the jerk I have been."

"Forget the apology. It is just good to have you back," Seth told him.

Talking with Max that evening was different from before. When Rachel had first met Max and Seth in Issym, she had wondered why the two were friends; but now, she began to understand that there actually was a descent side to Max, one that the teen promised would become more prominent.

Seeing a long lost person made Rachel realize just how much she had missed the twins, Mary and Elise. *How am I ever going to get them home?*

Smolden and his men arrived at Kembar plains, where Sasha was already waiting for them. "Did you get the gem of light?" Smolden asked Sasha.

"Of course I did," Sasha snapped, leaning against a boulder.

"Where is it?"

"Hidden. Don't worry; it's safe. This way I'll know that I can trust you to keep up your end of the bargain," she lied.

"Fine," Smolden answered, contented with the knowledge that he would soon be able to dispose of her. "But I won't give you eternal youth until you give me the gem."

"That was not part of our original bargain!" Sasha protested, now standing straight up. "I brought Seth to Issym so I have already earned eternal youth. I help you conquer Issym and then we co-rule. That was the deal. Me getting the gem of light for you was a bonus. You should thank me, not force me to hand it over. If I hadn't retrieved it, you would be dead by now. After all, your own domain collapsed on you!" Sasha laughed, taking great pleasure in mocking the beast.

Smolden let out a low growl. "Since you only half completed the first task and got Seth to Issym but not to me, I won't give eternal youth to you until after the battle."

Sasha was displeased, but she was confident she could come up with another way of getting what she wanted; she knew how to force the dragon's hand. She told Smolden, "I have an idea." Once she had explained it, she added, "I'll only do it if you give me the secret of eternal youth now."

"Alright," growled the leviathan, knowing that he was going to have to give a convincing lie. "Have it your way."

Chapter 28

More and more people were arriving in the land of the fairies and mushnicks every hour. Kate showed up with some airsprites. Rachel hurried over to them to find out how Mary and Elise were doing. Jennet informed her, "They are fine, but very homesick...more and more so as each day passes."

Much to Seth and Rachel's surprise, they were not summoned to any meeting that morning. Just before lunch, Elimelech came over to them, "Our king asked me to tell you that the army will be leaving tomorrow. We are going to battle Smolden's army at Kembar plains."

"Was there another meeting this morning? Why were we not sent for?" Seth questioned.

"We had to discuss things that were not for your ears."

Seth changed the topic, though every part of him wanted to know what he could not be trusted to know. "Why not let Smolden's army attack us here?"

"We thought it better to fight him on our terms rather than on his. Also, we have many people here who won't be involved in the battle and they need somewhere safe to stay. We must have a place to fall back to if necessary and..."

"Okay. Okay. I get it," Seth cut in.

"It's time you get a lesson in sword fighting," Elimelech declared.

Seth followed him until they came to a house with nothing but grass behind it. They entered and were greeting by a fairy woman and her three children—Elimelech's family. The fairy man took something from the far corner and then led Seth out the back door to the clearing.

"This," started Elimelech, showing Seth the wrapped object he had retrieved from the house, "was made for you."

The fairy man took off the cloth and revealed a broadsword, with a sliver handle and a shining, milky white blade. Seth stared, wondering why its radiance seemed so familiar. "The gem of light!" Seth cried. "I said that you should craft this blade and give it to a skilled fighter—not me."

"Who else could we give it to? Even with the sword a warrior would have to hit him in just the right spot to do any real damage. Who stands a better chance then you, who imagined him and know his weaknesses?"

"But I don't remember! And I am a terrible sword fighter."

"Perhaps the memories will return. We have made our choice; this is what we counseled about this morning. The sword is yours. You must take it."

Seth hesitated. He did not want this responsibility. He had no desire to be the hero that saved Issym... or died trying. And yet God had made his path very clear. This was his duty, whether he liked it or not. With determination, the teen reached out and grasped the weapon. It was surprisingly light.

"Let me teach you how to use that thing," Elimelech declared. For the next several hours, they practiced. Surprisingly, it did not take Seth long to master sword fighting. He had always imagined that he was good at it and thus, in Xsardis, he was. *Maybe I can do this after all,* thought Seth.

That night, Rachel brought Seth his dinner. "Thanks," he told her.

She made no reply and sat down on the other side of the small fire. She pulled her cloak closer around her shoulders and wrapped her arms around her knees.

"Something wrong?" Seth asked.

Rachel remained silent.

"Rachel, what's wrong?" questioned Seth for the second time. She still did not respond. "Tell me, already," Seth prodded.

Finally, she declared, "I saw you holding the gem sword. They want you to battle Smolden."

"Oh," Seth said quietly. "You don't think I can defeat him."

"Thinking about David fighting Goliath really puts me to shame. I always believed it; but what if it was just a story? Perhaps it was a parable, like Jesus told in the New Testament. I mean, what are we doing? These people think we're heroes! We're not..."

Seth looked up at the stars. He would never have guessed that Rachel would think like that. "You always seemed so sure that the stories were true..."

She buried her face, "I was... but here we are, Seth, and it's our lives on the line, and lives of all Issym. We're asking them to trust us, and we're going to let them down."

"Do you wonder if David felt the same way?"

Rachel glanced up, the fire reflecting off her eyes as she looked into Seth's. "What do you mean?"

"More than David's life was in danger. If he lost, all Israel became slaves. He surely seemed inadequate for the job. He was small, only a child. He took stones and a sling to fight a heavily armed giant. And the weight of all Israel was on his shoulders."

"How did he do it?" Rachel asked. "I always thought that in his place I would have done the same thing. Of course I would trust in God to protect me. But now, when it really comes to it, I don't know that I can."

"Have you noticed that when people here talk about Issym, they seem to think of him as a fearless warrior? That wasn't how I imagined him. When King Shobal recalled him to his home continent to join in a battle, Issym did not want to go. He was content for the first time in his life, having his purpose in caring for his kingdom and his joy in loving his wife. He was afraid of losing them.

"But Asandra was an amazing woman. She told him to go, because they both knew he *should* go. She trusted in God to protect Issym."

"What is faith if it isn't tested..." Rachel muttered.

"Huh?"

"It's something my Grandfather used to say. *What is faith if it is not tested?* Mine has been shaken, but I'm not defeated yet. Fight the dragon," her voice rose in intensity. "Fight him like David fought Goliath and like Asandra sent Issym away."

"Rachel..." his tone was nervous as if he had something to say that would not be received well.

"What?"

"I had a talk with Elimelech, Galen, Curt and the fairy king. We all agreed you have to stay here."

"What do you mean?"

"You can't go to Kembar plains"

"Why on Xsardis not?" Rachel had risen to her feet in fury.

Seth stood up. "If for some reason we don't succeed in our battle, Issym will need another plan—it will need one of its creators to help launch another attack. I have the gem sword—I have to go. That only leaves you. You know this world better than I do. I'm sure you'll think something up to save Issym."

"That's ridiculous!" Rachel protested. "If the entire army falls to the undergrounders there is no way we could stand up against Smolden and Sasha. I have no plans—I know nothing about Xsardis that can help us if that happens. We need every person we can get out on the battlefield! I'm a good archer.

"Ever since the first day we arrived in Issym," she continued, her voice softer, "these people have shown us great kindness. People like Flibbert risked their lives for us. People like Galen gave up their time to see us safely to our destination. People like Orvan gave up their most treasured possessions to help us. And so many others have given so much for us! Let me help them in whatever way I can. I've fallen in love with this world. Let me help!"

Seth was resolute, "The decision has been made. You can do the most for Issym by staying safe."

Chapter 29

As daylight rose, so rose the frogs, humans, mushnicks, illuminescents, airsprites, shape shifters, and fairies. Tension radiated through the camp. Battle was coming. Though the results might be favorable, many good creatures would die that day. No one spoke unless it was necessary. No one moved unless it was necessary.

Elimelech, Galen and Seth walked towards Rachel. "We have a problem," the fairy man started.

Rachel's face was grave, fully aware of what the day would bring, "What is it?"

"We can't speak to the illuminescents so we won't be able to tell them when to use their powers to stop Smolden from breathing fire," Seth answered.

Rachel smugly slung her quiver of arrows over her shoulder. "Then you'll need me to go with you."

"You planned this, didn't you?" Seth figured.

"I realized last night that you would need someone who could communicate with the illuminescents; since I am the only one who speaks their language, you will have to take me along."

"You can't go," Elimelech told her. "There's no question about that."

"What will you do without me? Seth said that I couldn't go because I would be of more help to Issym here, but now you need me on the battlefield."

"If you just teach the illuminescents one word of our language so that when they hear it they will activate their powers, we'll be fine without you," Galen responded.

Rachel fought back a scowl that threatened to overtake her face. She wanted to go; she could not accept that they were leaving her behind. It did not make any sense. But apparently it was not her call. "Fine. I'll tell the illuminescents that when they hear the word 'kiash' they are to stop Smolden from blowing fire."

"Kiash? Galen said a word of *our* language," Seth replied.

"It is," Galen put in. "At least, it is in Issym. 'Kiash' means victory, but its more than that. It's almost like a prayer to God to bring victory, and faith that He will."

Elimelech added, "Everyone knows the word, but people don't use it anymore. They just say 'victory'. Using 'kiash' is a wise choice. You can be sure that no one will say it until one of the leaders shouts it. Then everyone will join in."

Rachel told Ruby what had been decided and the illuminescent went off to tell her people.

Before the sun was high enough to cast shadows and while bones still shook with the cold of night, creatures of all kinds could be seen saying their goodbyes to those staying behind.

Princess Valerie and Rachel watched as Seth rode off in the lead of the army with Curt, Elimelech, Flibbert, the fairy king and Galen. Max and Prince Aldair rode close behind.

The princess told her, "My brother wouldn't let me go. He said somebody would have to watch over the kingdom if he…" her voice trailed off. "I've never been good with a sword or bow anyway."

Rachel and Valerie did not move until the last of the soldiers had disappeared from sight. The army marched through the morning and stopped behind a hill overlooking Kembar plains. Seth and other leaders climbed to the top of the hill. They hid behind a thick group of trees, wanting to look over Smolden's forces for themselves. The army of light outnumbered the army of darkness by a couple hundred, but they knew that the latter army had a huge dragon and a multiplying shape shifter on its side.

Seth caught his first glance of Smolden. The mighty beast ripped a tree from the ground with one four-clawed foot and tossed it aside like a doll. His glistening onyx scales were both terrifying and beautiful. Pointed, silver spikes ran up and down his back. Though it was daylight, darkness appeared to cover the area around the dragon. Surely this beast was evil, but how could Seth destroy Smolden, his brainchild, his creation, something so powerful and magnificent? The teen shuddered. What was he thinking? He grasped at the hilt of the gem sword. His mission was clear and he would complete it.

Galen tapped the teen's shoulder and whispered, "I saw movement there. It must be one of Smolden's scouts. Within minutes he'll know that we're here."

Elimelech waited the appropriate amount of time and declared, "Something is wrong. Smolden's army is too small. He must know that we are here. Sasha should have multiplied by now."

Kate moved towards them. "I cannot feel any shape shifter presences," she informed them. "Sasha is not here."

"What could that mean?" inquired Seth.

Elimelech's voice was grave, "Worse case scenario: Sasha is on her way to the land of the mushnicks and fairies. All of our fighters are here. If Sasha really is heading there, our people don't stand a chance."

"What do we do?" Seth's body tensed. Sasha would massacre the people.

"There's not much we can do. We cannot spare any men."

"So, we're not going to do anything?" Seth could not believe it and he would not stand for it. "I'm no war leader, but that is not an acceptable plan."

"Let all of my shape shifters go back to the land of the mushnicks and fairies," Kate suggested. "There is still some frog armor there, which makes it possible to kill shape shifters. We are Sasha's kind and we are the best ones to stand up to her."

"Sasha could multiply herself beyond what you can defeat with your small number," Flibbert warned her.

"I can handle Sasha," Kate reassured and headed off to gather her people.

Seth looked back over the plains where the battle would soon take place. The wide, empty space was encircled by trees; there would be plenty of room to fight. He glanced back at Smolden and bit his lip to send away his nerves. *Lord, help us,* he prayed.

Elimelech said, "The illuminescents are going to stay hidden in the woods until we call for them. We should try not to use their powers until we absolutely need them. Everyone knows that if they hear someone yelling 'kiash' they should join in."

"Okay," Seth replied, not really listening.

"Are you ready for this?"

"Probably not, but I'd rather not sit here thinking about it."

They descended the hill and retrieved their horses. Then, raising a shout, the army of light charged their enemies. The undergrounders were prepared for their attack. The fighting began.

Flibbert was the first to meet the enemy. No one who knew the frog was surprised by this. Seth urged his horse on towards Smolden. Galen stayed near by the teen, attempting to ensure that Seth stayed alive long enough to face the leviathan.

As Seth closed the distance between himself and Smolden, he felt his horse sway beneath him. It collapsed, throwing him from it. A minotaur swung his ax towards Seth's head before the teen could gain his feet. Galen saved the his life by tackling the undergrounder to the ground. Without standing, Seth plunged his dagger into the beast's heart, hardly believing what he had done.

He sat there, unable to move. "Seth, snap out of it. There's no time for this!" Galen hollered. The teen stood, pulling his dagger out of the minatour. He wanted to keep the gem sword sheathed, so that Smolden would not know about the weapon until it was absolutely necessary.

The leviathan was now in the air, reigning down fire upon his enemies and his allies alike. As Seth watched Smolden wreak havoc, he was shocked to see that the great beast showed no concern whatsoever if he burned his own men. Within minutes, Seth heard Elimelech shout out, "Kiash!" Seth joined in the cry and so did others.

The illuminescents moved out of the woods like a swarm of bees. It did not take long for Seth to see results. Smolden had been in the middle of a breath of fire, but the flame simply ceased. Baffled, the dragon descended to the ground.

Seth raced towards Smolden; now would be the best time for their duel. The teen was not yet worn from battle; the dragon was in a state of bewilderment from the illuminescents. Seth neared the creature's leg and dropped his dagger. He reached for the gem sword. Out of the corner of his eye, the teen saw a human undergrounder charging at him. He ducked to avoid his sword. When he looked up again, Smolden was gone. Seth turned his attention back to his human assailant, who was readying another attack. Flibbert stepped in front of him. "Get to Smolden!" the frog shouted.

The leviathan had descended at one of the edges of the battle. Seth struggled just to keep his footing. The two hours during which Smolden was not able to breath fire were expiring, but the teen could not get near him.

The noise of the battle was deafening, so loud that Seth could hardly distinguish the dragon's roar. Creatures fighting and dying and falling and rising filled every scrap of land. There was no time for fear, and yet how could one not be afraid?

As Seth did his best to contribute to the battle, he began to see the people of Issym with greater respect. Green fairies used their powers to break through shields. Frogs jump-kicked their opponents. Airsprites flew archers above the fray. Illuminescents concentrated their efforts on holding back Smolden's fire. Humans fought hard and bravely. He could not let these creatures down.

Smolden was not able to breathe fire, but he could bite, stomp and swing his tail. Even with the dragon's handicap, he was measurably reducing the number of the army of light every minute.

Seth knew he did not have much time. If he could not get to Smolden, maybe he could get Smolden to come to him. Saying a quick prayer, he drew the gem sword. As he held it up, a brilliant light flashed. It must have been more than the sun's reflection. Smolden roared in pain and undergrounders covered their eyes, but Seth's fellows were encouraged and doubled their attack.

Smolden comprehended the threat, and within seconds he descended before Seth, "Drop the sword, boy. You don't know what you're doing."

"I won't quit until you are dead!" Seth shouted over the din of the battle.

"I can send you home. Just drop the sword. Don't make me kill you."

"There's a story in the Bible, Smolden," Seth called. The battle sounds seemed to be fading in the background, and time appeared to have stopped. "About a little boy who had to fight a giant. God gave him the strength to win the battle."

"Your God can't help you here!" spat Smolden.

"You're wrong. That's what the giant said, but now he is dead. God gave the boy victory over Goliath and He will give me victory over you!" Seth cried out, charging towards Smolden. He slashed the beast's leg, drawing blood, but the leviathan showed no sign of pain. Smolden kicked Seth and sent him flying. The teen landed with a thud, air knocked out of him. He got back up quickly and jabbed at the other leg. This time Seth dodged the dragon's kick.

The teen saw illuminescents fleeing from the battle. Smolden felt the ability to breath fire return. As the dragon drew in a breath to exhale flame, Seth ran underneath him, stabbing at his belly and then his hind legs. No matter where Seth hit the dragon, he could not find a spot that seemed to weaken Smolden.

Sasha was running in the shape of a lion towards the land of the fairies and mushnicks, while the undergrounders fought at Kembar plains. This was the idea she had talked about with Smolden. The fact was, Sasha could not care less about co-ruling Issym. Her primary target was Asandra. From there she would begin her world empire.

Sasha had only agreed to fight with Smolden because she wanted the secret to living forever.

Smolden had told her of a well on Norick, an island off the coast of Asandra, which would give eternal youth. She hoped he was not lying. Ordinarily she would have made certain he wasn't before doing her part. Now, however, she had a target, Rachel, whom she could not afford to underestimate and who had to be killed quickly.

Rachel was the only one who could stop her from taking Asandra. The teenager had created the continent and knew everything about it. Unlike Seth, who had forgotten his creations, Rachel still imagined and thus was a formidable enemy. But the girl's flaws were numerous—the biggest one being her obedience. Sasha knew the fairies would never let the teen go to war, and Rachel would comply with their command. Idiot. It would be the death of her. Sasha would never have been left behind. She would have led the way into battle. That was why she was destined to rule and Rachel was destined to die.

Chapter 30

Sasha felt a shape shifter coming towards her. The next thing she knew, a cheetah was tackling her. The animal took on the form a human. "Kate," spat Sasha as she took on her own preferred human form.

"What are you up to, Sasha?" Kate replied.

"Get out of my way. You can't stop me."

She's right. I can't stop her; but I can slow her down, thought Kate. The other shape shifters were going to head straight to the land of the fairies and warn the people there that Sasha was on her way. Kate needed to slow her enemy down as much as she could.

Sasha morphed into a leopard and headed away. Kate followed as a cheetah and tackled her again. Sasha turned into a falcon and Kate turned into a hawk, flying at her enemy. Sasha stayed as a falcon but also became a bear. Kate stayed as a hawk, but, to Sasha's surprise, also became a wall, which the bear could not scale. *Kate, too, can be in different forms at once!* Sasha could have screamed. "I have underestimated you," Sasha admitted as she formed into a human on the other side of the wall. Kate formed another wall, in response.

In this way, Kate delayed Sasha's arrival by about two hours.

Suddenly Seth thought, *His eyes. He's got to be weak enough there that I can get my blade through his eye and into his brain.* Seth began to formulate a plan. *His head is big enough for me to stand on, but then I'd have to get on his head...How in Issym am I going to do that? The hill! I could climb to the top of the hill, which is about the same size as the dragon; then I could jump on Smolden's head, and stab him in the eye.* It was a ludicrous plan, Seth had to admit, but what choice did he have?

Seth tried to get to the hill but Smolden's tail whipped around and blocked the teen's path. Seth dropped to the ground and rolled to his right to escape the dragon's foot. *How am I going to get up the hill? Smolden isn't going to let me out of his sight for a moment.* Just then, Seth saw Galen fighting not far from him. "Galen!" he called.

The man worked his way over to Seth, who was losing strength from trying not to be burnt, bitten or stomped on by the dragon or attacked from any undergrounders around him. The teen was running out of energy, but so was Smolden. The gem slowed his movements, if only a little. "I need your help to kill Smolden," Seth told Galen. "I want you to distract him long enough for me to get up the hill. Then, let him come after me and I'll jump on his head."

Galen, blocking yet another undergrounder attack, gave Seth a strange look, but only said, "Give me a few minutes."

"I'll try." Seth did not know if he could. His strength was almost gone. He could not get out of the way of the dragon's next kick. Smolden's leg rammed against him, sending him backwards. Seth landed face first. The pain in his arm told him it was broken. He tasted blood in his mouth. His whole body screamed at him and he struggled to keep consciousness.

The teen knew that if he did not move, Smolden would surely crush him. He managed to roll over. Smolden stood over Seth. Was the dragon actually grinning? "I told you your God couldn't help you," the beast rasped.

For one small second Seth was sure he was going to die, but then Smolden let out a roar and turned his head in the direction of his tail. Galen and seven others had jumped on it and were holding on for dear life. Seth smiled as he stood. He was bruised, he was battered, his arm was broken, and he should be dead; but God had not abandoned him. Seth had no strength, but he would have shamed a trained sprinter as he ran to the hill, not once glancing behind him.

As he climbed the knoll, Seth looked at Smolden's tail. Only Galen and one other man were left hanging on. Seth climbed faster. He was half way up when the dragon finally dislodged the last of his assailants and surged towards Seth. Smolden would reach the hill before Seth had made it to the top.

What now? Seth prayed. *You've had a plan this far, God.* He continued to climb and looked at the dragon. He saw one human jump onto Smolden's tail. The dragon's balance was disrupted, and he stopped moving to throw the man off. Seth could not believe his eyes. It was Max who had jumped on the leviathan's tail.

Max managed to hold on long enough for Seth to reach the top; then Smolden flung him from his tail and charged towards the hill. Seth took a deep breath. *This is it,* he thought. *I have one chance to jump from the hill onto the dragon. Oh God, please help me make it.* Seth got a running start and flung himself towards Smolden. He landed hard on the dragon's snout, causing pain to rush through his broken arm.

Smolden stopped moving. His two eyes tried to focus on Seth. The teen straightened himself with a groan and plunged the gem sword deep into Smolden's right eye. The blade remained embedded, even when Seth withdrew his hand and stood, teetering, on the dragon's snout.

For one breathless moment nothing happened. Then suddenly Smolden's body began to sway back and forth. Seth was thrown through the air again, and this time the pain of the impact was too great for his body. He lost consciousness and did not see the leviathan fall to the ground, never to rise again.

A great cheer rose from the army of light. Most of the undergrounders immediately turned and headed for the woods. Their undefeatable master was defeated. Not every undergrounder, however, was ready to be done fighting.

Max had not yet gained his footing after being thrown from Smolden's tail. A toad neared him and brought his sword in the direction of Max's heart. Out of the corner of his eye, the teen saw Prince Aldair come charging toward the toad. He tackled the undergrounder.

The toad plunged a dagger he had had around his waste into Aldair's chest, but that did not stop the prince. Aldair cut off the toad's head.

"Arvin!" Max shouted as his friend toppled to the ground.

"Max," Aldair grabbed Max's shoulder as the teen knelt beside him. "Tell Valerie that she... will make a great... ruler of the castle," the prince spoke softly and slowly, coughing in between every few words. "And tell Curt... that I have always appreciated his friendship. And you, Max..."

"You can give them those messages yourself. We will get a healing fairy to help you," Max cut in.

"Fairies aren't God... They can't heal everything. Don't loose... that newfound faith in God. He...." Aldair's words died out, but he kept his hand on Max's shoulder.

"Thank you," Max told him, "for not giving up on me when I was helping Smolden. Thank you for giving your life for mine."

"God has a purpose for you. I have served mine. I now get to go home." The prince's eyes sparkled with expectation as he breathed his last.

Fairies of the blue scattered throughout Kembar plains, healing the wounded. Max summoned them to Prince Aldair, but he knew that there was nothing they could do.

The blue fairies healed the wounded, including Seth, as the rest of the army of Issym chased down the undergrounders. When the soldiers returned to the Kembar plains, they prepared to spend the night. They would travel home the next morning.

Seth and Max, sitting beside a fire, breathed a sigh of relief. The battle was over—or was it? They had no way to know what was going on in the land of the fairies and mushnicks.

Chapter 31

Rachel was helping some mushnick women prepare dinner when a green illuminescent showed up in the entrance to the cottage. The way he hovered in the doorway made her certain that the news he was bringing was bad. "What is going on?" Rachel asked him.

"Sasha the shape shifter is on her way here right now. Smolden and the rest of the army are staying at Kembar plains, but Sasha is coming," the little illuminescent replied.

Rachel turned to one of the mushnick women, only then realizing that no one had understood the creature's message but her, "Nancy, get your husband. We have a problem."

Those still in the land of the fairies and mushnicks prepared for Sasha's arrival. They put on what armor was left and equipped themselves with the few swords around. The mushnicks quickly made more arrows for the remaining bows and turned some of their farming equipment into weapons.

Rachel grabbed her bow and some arrows and, like the other archers, hid herself in the trees. Everyone else, including the swordsmen, stood inside the houses, praying and waiting.

Almost two hours later some ally shape shifters showed up. They reaffirmed that Sasha was on her way.

Within the hour that followed, Sasha appeared. She had multiplied herself into a hundred different looking forms. It was difficult for the defenders of the land of the mushnicks and fairies to distinguish which forms were Sasha and which were their own allies.

The defenders didn't want to battle their fellows so they would not attack; they would only defended themselves. This gave Sasha the advantage. But the stone of the frog armor made it so that when one version of Sasha fell, it could not rematerialize.

Almost every shot Rachel took hit its mark. The other archers were just as good, if not better. Eventually Rachel ran out of arrows. Since she and the other archers could do no more, they stayed in their trees and watched as Sasha started to lose the battle. One by one the shifter's forms died.

Finally an old fairy of the blue shouted, "It's alright friends. It's over. Sasha is dead." Rachel wondered how they could be absolutely certain, but no one was fighting so she figured it was safe to come out of her tree.

The creatures in the land of the fairies and mushnicks began to see to the wounded. The versions of Sasha that had died disappeared all at once, leaving only the noble creatures in the area. The versions of Kate and the good shifters that had died disappeared as well.

Rachel shuddered as she saw some mushnicks being carried off to be buried. How could anyone want to be queen enough to kill these playful creatures for it?

Rachel, like most of the others, spent the night without sleep. Only a few fairies of the blue were still in the land of the fairies and mushnicks and their abilities were limited. Many of the wounded had to heal on their own. The victorious defenders spent the night cleaning wounds, administering medicines and feeding the injured.

Daylight came, and still no one slept. Noon rolled around and the mushnick named Nancy sent Rachel to the main building to get some of the medicines the fairies kept there. Rachel found them in the back of the circular building, just where Nancy had said they would be. She grabbed the bag of medicines and headed for the door.

Suddenly she heard cheering. Could the army be home? Rachel's face lit up as she quickened her step. The cheering grew louder. The army was definitely home.

As Rachel neared the door it opened, and a woman stepped inside, letting the door close behind her. "Is the army home?" the teen inquired.

"Yes," she answered

"I can't wait to see them." Rachel moved to the left of the woman and stepped towards the door, already thinking about greeting her friends and worrying about any who might not have returned.

The woman blocked her path, "But I'm afraid, my dear, that you won't be able to see them."

"Why on Xsardis not?"

The woman spoke in cool tones, "Because you are not going to make it out of this building alive."

A shiver ran up Rachel's spine and she began to back away.

A sinister smile grew across the woman's face. "You thought I was dead, but I am not. And now I am not going to let you live. Smolden's power may have been overcome, but I will *never* be defeated."

Rachel took a breath. It made sense. Sasha would have been smart enough not to let every version of herself die. "What is it that you want?"

"To be ruler of Asandra, of course. While you and your friends were defending Issym, Asandra has been falling into my hands. Its capital city will be the base for my world empire." Sasha pulled a dagger from her ankle and moved towards Rachel.

"The only reason I was helping Smolden was to get the secret of eternal youth," she continued. "Now that I have that, I'll head to Asandra. With you dead—you who know Asandra so well—no one will be able to keep me from taking all that I desire."

"So you don't even care that we saved Issym?" Rachel questioned, still slowly moving backwards. She wanted to keep Sasha talking. The army of light was just outside. Perhaps someone would come looking for her.

"Actually, you did me a favor."

"What?" she whispered.

"I needed Smolden to be killed, and now he is. With you and him dead, nothing stands in my way."

Rachel's back was against the wall now—there was nowhere else to go. Her hope and courage were failing. There was no one looking for her, no help coming, no way to defend herself and Sasha's dagger was moving ever closer to her heart. Issym was safe—the battle was over—but she was about to die.

There was a great welcome for the army when it returned to the land of the fairies and mushnicks. Sorrow and joy were mingled together on everyone's faces as they reunited. Max, like so many others, had the difficult job of letting someone know that a person they loved had died. Max approached Princess Valerie. The woman knew from the teen's face what had happened. Tears swelled up in her eyes. They mourned together.

It seemed like everyone wanted to shake Seth's hand, but the one he most wanted to see had not appeared to greet him. After several minutes, he grew concerned. As he heard some of the mushnicks talk about the battle with Sasha, he feared Rachel had died; but one mushnick told him, with a large grin and enthusiastic gestures, "Oh, she made it through! The last I saw her, she was headed over towards the main building." Seth dodged the congratulators of various species and headed straight for the building. His heart knew something was wrong.

He swung open the door. A woman had a dagger aimed at Rachel's heart. The door clunked shut behind him and the woman turned to face Seth, "This is better than I could have hoped for," she declared, stepping towards Seth. "Killing you will ensure my reign over Issym too."

Hope bloomed in Rachel. She thought, *Sasha is distracted by Seth. There has to be something I can do.*

On a wall not many feet away from Rachel hung a bow and an arrow, looking old and costly, more like ancient artifacts than weapons.

The bow was made of a substance like ivory and the arrow appeared to have been formed from the scales of a dragon. Could this be the same weapon that the fairy Elaine had given her in the stories from her childhood?

As Sasha stepped towards Seth, Rachel snatched the bow, notched the arrow, aimed and released. Sasha collapsed to the ground.

Both Seth and Rachel had lost all color. Her hands shook as she let the bow fall to the ground. He walked past Sasha's lifeless body and put his arms around his friend. They had been through a lot. They were ready to go home. "Are you okay?" he asked, letting her go.

"Yeah. You?" Rachel responded.

"Yes."

Rachel noticed that something had fallen from Sasha's pocket. The object was round and wrapped in a white cloth. Rachel carefully unwrapped the item. Both of their eyes lit up. "Universe Girl's missing orb," Seth breathed.

"Home. This is how we get home." Their nightmare was almost over. But had it really been a nightmare?

They had met so many good people. Thoughts of Orvan, Galen, Flibbert, shape shifters, fairies, mushnicks, airsprites and illuminescents flooded their minds. Their time in Issym had been a struggle, but it had been worth it. They had not only helped Issym— Issym had helped them.

Seth and Rachel relayed their encounter with Sasha and the discovery of Universe Girl's orb to their friends outside.

The war had passed and a great celebration had begun. Fires were started, music was played, food was brought. Joyous laughter could be heard throughout the camp.

Darkness set in the land, but the fires lit their ongoing festivities. "Rachel!" two little voices shouted over the music. The teen turned around and was knocked off her feet by the tackling hugs of Mary and Elise. Seth saw another familiar face approaching them— Universe Girl, or Ethelwyn, as she liked to be called.

Seth and Rachel heard someone shout for silence and then saw the fairy king fly into the air so that all could see him. "When I was a young lad I told my father I did not want to be king. He asked me why.

I told him that I would not be a very good king. I was not an Issym or a hero, but today, people of Issym, we see that heroes are not those who have no fear and who always know what is right. Heroes can be the most unlikely people. They may not always feel equal to the task, but they put aside their wishes and strive to do what is right.

"Today we have among us such heroes. Seth, Rachel, and Max, by the will of God, and with the help of all of you who have struggled at their sides, have saved Issym from the mighty dragon Smolden and the evil shape shifter Sasha." The people of Issym let out a great cheer.

As the roar of the crowd subsided, the king continued, "But now it is time for our heroes to go home." Every eye turned towards Seth, Rachel, Max, Mary and Elise.

Ethelwyn extended her hand for her orb. As Seth presented the sphere, it leapt from his hand and hovered above her open palm. Other orbs joined the one in dancing in circles around her, growing closer together as they made their way upwards. After a few moments they joined together, forming a vast, radiant sphere around Ethelwyn. Then the newly formed orb slowly descended to the ground, with Universe Girl in its center. "Seth and Max, when you're ready, stand over there," she instructed as she pointed to a certain spot. "You will go home first."

Seth looked around. How could ever he say goodbye to all these people?

Galen, Flibbert and Princess Valerie approached. "Thank you for everything." Flibbert spoke to both Seth and Max. Max was surprised that the frog had spoken to him—they had never been on good terms.

Max turned towards the princess. What she whispered to him no one heard, but the teen seemed to have a look of honor, hope and determination on his face after her words. He realized in that moment that another's life had bought his own. He would use his life well to honor that gift.

"Keep out of trouble," Galen told Seth.

"Goodbye," Seth answered. It was such a pathetic word. It could not express all he had on his mind—no words, however many, could.

Seth turned to Rachel. "I still live in the same house," she told him. "Look me up."

"Oh, I will," he answered, looking her in the eyes.

"It was nice to have met you Max," Rachel added as he and Seth walked to the spot Ethelwyn had directed.

"You as well," Max replied.

Inside the big orb, Universe Girl touched a galaxy, a planet, a continent, and so forth. When she was finished, a bright light gleamed from the sphere. And Seth and Max disappeared.

Rachel, Mary, and Elise stepped up to the orb, waving goodbye to Flibbert and Galen. Ethelwyn repeated the process with slight modifications, and with a flash, they vanished as well.

After Seth, Rachel, Max, Mary and Elise went home, Galen wasted no time. He got together a small army and headed for Mt. Smolden. Even with the dragon dead, the towns surrounding Mt. Smolden would not be safe until the mountain was purged from the evildoers who called it their home.

Epilogue

"Do you think Seth and Rachel and Max will ever come back to Xsardis?" Joppa's niece questioned as he closed the book.

"I wish I knew," the old man answered.

"I hope they do. Sometimes I dream about meeting them."

Joppa was hardly listening to the girl. He was more focused on the sounds of intruders searching the forest above them. They would not stop until they had found him; he could not let them discover his niece or his hideout. The self-professed queen feared knowledge above all else. Joppa had much wisdom and history compiled in his home. If the queen found it... Joppa shuddered. And what if she found his niece? The queen would try to use her to get the old man to betray Asandra.

"I pray they return," he told the eleven-year-old. "They may be our only hope."

Preview Chapter 1 of the next book in the Xsardis Chronicles,

Asandra

...

Asandra

by

Jessie Mae Hodsdon

Chapter 1

They moved with joint precision. Running through the forest with a silent haste, the two teenagers increased the distance between them and their pursuers. As soon as they were certain that they were out of sight, the boy dropped to the ground and opened a hatch that was covered with plant life. The girl hopped into it and he followed, pulling the leafy cover over them.

The two stopped moving and tried not to breathe. Their enemy passed above them, but did not stop. "That was a close one," the teenage girl almost shouted with enthusiasm. She seemed to enjoy danger.

"Mom is going to kill us..." the boy murmured.

"Come on, Ev. You didn't find that even a little fun?" his sister teased, punching him on the shoulder.

He shook his head.

"Don't look so nervous," she chastised. "We're safe now."

They stood and began to walk through the tunnel. It grew so dark that the boy could not distinguish the form of his sister, but they continued without slowing their pace. They knew these passages well. Finally, after a series of twists and turns, they saw light in the distance. The tunnel widened to make a room, lit by torches with three openings leading away. A raggedly dressed guard stood in front of each one. The sentry moved aside as they entered the leftmost way.

After passing a series of doors, the siblings took another left and two more guards stepped aside to allow them entrance to the room behind them. As they stepped in and closed the door, they saw yet again how small the apartment was. It had a torn rug lying on the floor, torches on the walls, a bed, a desk and a chair. It was by far the nicest room in the underground, but even so...

A woman sat in the chair, leaning on her desk as she supported her head with her hand. At the sounds of the teens, she turned around to face them. Her dress was pristine; her brown hair was curled and long, with a slender crown upon her head. She would have been strikingly beautiful if concern had not aged her before her time. Looking at them she guessed, "Had a close encounter with Sasha's men?"

"Yes Mother," the boy replied, ready to get the truth out in the open.

"How close Evan?" she asked.

"They did not discover our hiding place," Evan replied; that was what truly mattered.

"But they *almost* did," she surmised. "And what would have happened if they had? How foolish! You insist that I let you go above, but you almost got us discovered."

She shook her head and the weight of her hair left it unmoved as she continued, "We are not just ordinary rebels. I am the rightful queen; you are the prince and princess. If we get caught, what do you think will happen to the resistance?" Her tone was harsh, but they knew that it was only her concern for them and the others in the hiding place that made her speak so. She sighed, "Did you get what you were looking for, Katerina?"

Katerina's face lit up. In truth she had not been listening—she had heard enough lectures to have them bounce right off. She opened up the muddy bag she wore around her shoulder and pulled out a red gem on a string. "I'm so glad Ian kept it hidden for me. I thought I had lost it."

Evan and Katerina had each been given a gift on the day of their birth—Katerina's was a chord with a ruby on it and tethered under Evan's shirt was a large blue gem. Katerina returned her stone to its rightful place on her neck and fingered it. Queen Juliet had given Evan his and King Remar had bestowed Kat with hers. Oh how the princess missed her father! He had been captured by Sasha, the wicked shape shifter, years and years ago. Her father had always listened to her, always loved her, always cared for her. Katerina thanked the stars that he had been wearing commoner's clothing the day he had been taken—Sasha had no idea that he was the king.

The queen called her children to her side. Wrapping an arm around each one she told them, "For many days I have fasted and prayed and I have come to this conclusion. You must go to earth and bring us back Rachel and Seth, the ones who imagined Xsardis."

Katerina's face was a mixture of shock and awe.

"But how will we get to earth?" questioned the ever sensible Evan. To him it was a logical conclusion. To her, it was a more adventurous decision than she had ever seen her mother make.

"Katerina, hand me your necklace," Juliet commanded.

Kat hesitated, but obeyed. Her mother put it on her desk. Taking a hammer she aimed for the ruby.

"What are you doing?" Kat shouted.

"You must trust me."

"Smash Evan's!" she protested.

"Your brother's is less powerful."

She brought the hammer down and the ruby shattered into pieces. Kat's heart filled with despair, feeling as if she had lost the last part of her father. Then anger took over. How could her mother have done it? Both emotions were suppressed as curiosity took their places.

Something was rising from the pieces. It looked like a red, glowing light. The light was smaller than her hand and it floated around the room, as if it were alive.

"What is it?" Katerina asked in wonder, as the creature started to buzz.

"An illuminescent."

"I thought those were just legends," Evan replied, flicking his eyes towards his mother for a moment and then turning his attention back to the creature.

"No," answered Juliet, "they are quite real, but as far as we know, the one you now see and the one in your gem, Evan, are the only ones to have survived."

The queen buzzed something to the illuminescent and it showered Kat and Evan with light. The next time they heared its sound, the teens thought it was trying to communicate something like, "Where am I?"

"There are different types of illuminescents," their mother explained, "but red ones have always belonged with royalty and they have the most extensive powers. Whereas the others only have one ability, red illuminescents have many."

"What can it help us do?"

"She can take you and your brother to earth."

Kat looked towards her mother with anticipation on her face, "When can we leave?"

Evan did not look as enthusiastic. The queen asked her son, "Why so reserved?"

"Because I know that this task will not be as easy as it sounds."

"True. Earth is not the same as Asandra. Your trip will be difficult and dangerous. Your task will take time, time that Asandra does not have. The longer you're there, the more established Sasha will become. And yet I can offer you very little guidance of how to begin your search. Rely upon your illuminescent. She will adapt more quickly to the new environment, but keep her safe, for she will be unable to blend in. Do not disclose your identities; do not say where you are from. You'll begin your search in New York City, New York. That's where Seth lives. Find him and he'll help you find Rachel. Remember to hurry."

The queen hugged each of her children. Katerina broke away quickly, but Evan lingered, trying to pass on some strength. Part of him knew that as dangerous as his trip was, it was more dangerous for his mother who was staying on Asandra.

"How does getting to earth work?" the princess asked.

"Ask your illuminescent. You need to learn to understand each other."

Kat looked towards Evan as if commanding him to talk to the creature. "Can you take us to earth?" he tried to say. He had never been much of a communicator in his own language, let alone an entirely new one.

"Yes."

"What do we need to do?" inquired Kat.

Without answering, the illuminescent hovered above them, showering them with red light. They disappeared.

Adventure with a purpose

Rebirth Publishing, Inc is committed to using adventurous literature and high quality writing to shine Christ in a dark world.

About the author:

Jessie Mae Hodsdon lives in Bangor, Maine where she serves in her church and community. She is currently finishing up her senior year of high school.